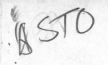

INSIDE PASSAGE TO DEATH

Leonie was recuperating from a painful divorce when her father, Judge John Warwick, booked passage for the family on a cruise of Alaska's Inside Passage. He had recently sentenced Mafia chieftain Alfredo Petrosino to jail, and needed a vacation to escape the publicity generated by the Mafia boss's threats against his life. But once underway, Leonie learned of Petrosino's escape, and two mysterious men began following her every move. Soon she found herself helplessly entangled in a web of danger and deceit as she struggled to save her father's life—and her own.

INSIDE PASSAGE TO DEATH

Mickey Lanford

ATLANTIC LARGE PRINT
Chivers Press, Bath, England.
Curley   Publishing,   Inc.,
South Yarmouth, Mass., USA.

Library of Congress Cataloging-in-Publication Data

Lanford, Mickey.
   Inside passage to death / Mickey Lanford.—Large print ed.
     p. cm.—(Atlantic large print)
   "An Atlantic book."
   ISBN 0–7927–0302–2 (soft: lg. print)
   1. Large type books. I. Title.
PS3562.A48466I57   1990
813′.54—dc20   90–34154
                                                      CIP

British Library Cataloguing in Publication Data

Lanford, Mickey
   Inside passage to death.
   I. Title
   813.54 [F]

   ISBN 0–7451–9843–0
   ISBN 0–7451–9855–4 pbk

This Large Print edition is published by Chivers Press, England, and
Curley Publishing, Inc, U.S.A. 1990

Published by arrangement with Dorchester Publishing Co., Inc

U.K. Hardback ISBN 0 7451 9843 0
U.K. Softback ISBN 0 7451 9855 4
U.S.A. Softback ISBN 0 7927 0302 2

INSIDE PASSAGE TO DEATH

CHAPTER ONE

INITIATE...
to begin or originate.

They were packing the last of the Waterford crystal when a riveting burst of sound penetrated the lush quiet of the elegant apartment.

'That sounded like gunfire!' Leonie Warwick's amber-flecked green eyes grew round in shocked disbelief.

'It certainly did,' her mother agreed. 'Is that possible?'

'In this day and time anything's possible.' Leonie's shrug reflected resignation and the weary acceptance of a sinful world. It said much for her present state of mind that she was more concerned with her own miseries than with someone else's problem.

Sanna Warwick teetered to the window on stiletto heels as Leonie repressed a smile at the sight of her petite mother eternally trying to make herself appear taller.

'It wasn't over in the park,' Sanna said. 'Too bad we can't see the street from here.' She shrugged, dismissing the improbable, then turned back to Leonie. 'How are we going to get all this downstairs?'

'Oh, that's all arranged. We'll carry what

we can and get help with the rest. Mike, the doorman, has a nephew who's always eager to earn some money to support his habit.' She had to laugh as Sanna's eyebrows flew upward. 'No, not drugs. Girls. And gasoline for those fancy wheels of his. I've seen that smashing blonde he's been trying to impress. No wonder he's always broke.' Leonie unconsciously put a hand to her own beautiful auburn hair as she moved toward the phone.

'Well, that's that,' she said after the arrangements had been made. 'Now I'll ...' She broke off as the nerve-rasping shriek of a siren developed rapidly, built to an almost unbearable crescendo, then stopped abruptly nearby. The two women looked at each other with the feeling of terrible foreboding that usually accompanies that ominous sound.

'That sounds as if it stopped right here! Perhaps that *was* gunfire we heard,' Leonie said, her green eyes wider than ever.

'Poor souls,' Sanna said compassionately. 'Whoever they are, I hope they can be helped.'

A vagrant sunbeam suddenly broke through the overcast sky as Leonie took up the last piece of crystal and it exploded into a dazzling shower of tiny rainbows. 'What a beautiful thing you are,' she murmured, then caught herself in horror. That was what Walter always said. And that had been the sum total of their brief but disastrous marriage. She was his beautiful possession, to be enjoyed at his pleasure.

In their tactful nonintrusive way, her parents had gently tried to suggest that she should not rush into marriage with a man she scarcely knew. But she wouldn't listen. From the first they had seen him for what he was: a calculating charmer spoiled by too much of everything—money, good looks, and women. He had wanted Leonie, and he was not used to being denied anything he wanted. It was only a minor annoyance that Leonie could be his only through marriage. He did not intend to let that change his lifestyle one bit.

In the early days it wasn't too hard to convince Leonie that she was the one who was lacking when she resisted his outrageous sexual demands on her. But by the time she realized how completely untrue that was, she was subjected to his brutality whenever she was slow or reluctant to comply. And he was quick to taunt her with accounts of the myriad other women who were only too happy to see things his way. The old sickness rose in her now at the memory.

'Tired, dear?' Sanna Warwick's feline eyes, so like her daughter's, held their usual look of anxiety as they searched Leonie's drawn face, mirroring her pain and heartache.

It's so unfair! Leonie thought in a burst of inward anger. Why should she pay for my stupidity too? Well, things are going to change. When we leave this place we're going to close the door forever on this part of my life. Starting now!

Her hands shook a little with the force of her emotion as she picked up her boxes and prepared to leave, but she summoned a smile and answered, 'I'm fine, Mother. Ready to go? Oh, don't forget Daddy's newspaper. I couldn't help wondering why you brought it over.'

'Oh!' Sanna slapped a slender hand to her forehead. 'Can you imagine? I forgot to show you the picture they took at the Arts Festival Ball. I think it turned out very well, don't you?'

'It's not bad,' Leonie admitted, then grimaced a little. 'But I'm afraid he'll send that foolish thing to everyone he knows.'

Sanna laughed. 'Don't spoil it for him. You know how proud he is of you.'

Leonie picked up the recent news edition. Her face softened as she looked at the photograph of her smiling father, standing straight and proud. The caption read: 'On the left, Judge John F. Warwick with his daughter, Leonie, as she accepts the award for the Arts Festival's Musician of the Year. Miss Warwick follows in the footsteps of her famous mother, the former concert pianist, Suzanna Waverly. Following this week's activities, the Warwicks soon plan to enjoy a

4

two-week cruise of Alaska's Inside Passage—a welcome change for the Judge after his masterful disposition of the sensational Petrosino trial.'

A welcome change for his daughter, too, Leonie thought grimly. From the much-envied socialite wife of a wealthy playboy back to the wholesome life of plain Leonie Warwick. She realized all too well she could never return to those pain-free days of innocence before her ill-fated marriage, but how good it would be to live as her own person again, free from fear. It was like being released from a particularly vile and brutal prison.

Another photograph caught her eye and she shuddered. Even a newspaper likeness could not mask the aura of pure menace that emanated from the face of Alfredo Petrosino. A shudder shook her again as she remembered the hoarse threats reverberating throughout the crowded courtroom as uniformed men dragged him away. What a frightening man! How could Dad have been so calm, so unafraid? He had sat there, unmoved, impressive in his strength and dignity. There was no gloating or rancor in his look, only an air of unspeakable weariness as he realized he had finally accomplished what so many before him had been unable—or unwilling—to do: pass sentence on one of the underworld's most dangerous men.

Leonie felt like ripping the front pages savagely from the newspaper, crumpling the hated face of Petrosino in a burst of fierce anger. How dare such filth vow vengeance against the finest, most honorable man in the world! But she managed to get her feelings under control and smiled at her mother as she said, 'I'm ready now.'

She stopped for one emotional moment, her hand on the doorknob, as vivid pictures flashed through her mind like full-color slides caught in the glare of a projector lamp. One of the brightest was that of Walter carrying her over this very threshold on their wedding night. All her romantic notions, all her unrealistic expectations gone—buried under pain and disillusionment. She sighed unconsciously as she prepared to close that chapter of her life and turn to a fresh page.

The street was crowded with morbidly curious onlookers, buzzing with the drama of violence. Sanna and Leonie found themselves promptly hemmed in, surrounded by restless bodies and the harsh breathing of excitement.

'What's happened? Do you think we can get back into the apartment?' Sanna asked anxiously. 'I can't even see if your car is at the curb.'

A commotion arose at some distance from them, and the crowd began to move somewhat, the murmur of sound rising to a clamorous level. The police were on the scene.

'Move on, please!' an authoritative voice ordered. 'There's nothing more to see. Clear the area. Let's move along now.'

'Nothing to see? Look at all that blood!' A harsh voice grated close to Leonie's ear.

The crush diminished and Leonie could see that her car was indeed standing at the curb. But she did not know how much longer she could stand practically immobile with the heavy box in her arms. She gasped and almost lost her balance as the heavyset man who matched the harsh voice jostled her rudely, exclaiming to his companion, 'A regular gangland execution! Did you see the bullet holes in those parked cars? It's a wonder they didn't kill somebody else. Much those types care. That's what happens when scum like that Petrosino can afford to live in this neighborhood. Bet you anything he's connected with this.'

'But he's in jail now,' the woman protested. 'They convicted him of just about every criminal activity anybody ever invented. And Judge Warwick sentenced him. I still can't believe it. He's gotten off so many other times.'

'You're right. I never thought I'd see the day. But he wouldn't do the job himself anyway; he'd assign it. Plenty of hatchetmen on the payroll.'

7

The couple finally moved on, opening a path to the curb, and Leonie let out an audible *whoosh* of relief. 'Come on, Mom,' she urged. 'I think we can get to the car now.'

'But we can't go anywhere yet,' Sanna argued. 'We're hemmed in.

'I know. But it's better than getting pushed around on the street. I'm about to drop my Waterford. To think I didn't want to trust it to the movers!'

'Oh, honey,' Sanna was instantly contrite. 'Would you believe I forgot it with all this mindboggling activity?'

The two women took advantage of the temporary opening and slipped gratefully into the big car. 'I'll just get in the back for now,' Leonie said. 'This box is so big, and there's no way I can get in on the driver's side. When the crowd's thinned out more I'll go and find Mike. He's not supposed to leave the door, of course, but I guess the excitement was too much for him.'

'I heard some of what that man said. Was there really some kind of gangster execution here?' Sanna was incredulous.

'I'm sure I don't know, Mom. I'm a lot taller than you, but I couldn't see anything either. It doesn't look too good for the victim, from what I was able to see. You can bleed to death in less than one minute if just one large artery is opened, you know. And from the look of things, someone's lost an incredible

8

amount of blood.'

Sanna looked at her curiously. 'You certainly pick up some odd bits of information,' she said.

Leonie laughed. 'I've learned a lot in my hospital volunteer work,' she said. One bit of information she did not feel it necessary to give was the fact that the notorious Alfredo Petrosino had been a neighbor.

They sat for some time then without speaking, pondering the dramatic event that had so brutally shattered the peace of this quiet and elegant neighborhood. Then Leonie jerked erect. 'The ambulance seems to be leaving. We ought to be able to go soon.'

She was upright, watching the emergency vehicle as it moved slowly down the congested street, siren wailing, trying to gather speed. She despised the ghoulish tendencies of others and was not particularly trying to look, but as the ambulance drew abreast she could see there was but one victim of the shooting. All the intent figures were grouped to the side nearest her car.

A large, dark-haired man, his business suit conspicuous among the blue-jacketed ambulance attendants, straightened up suddenly, allowing Leonie the briefest of glimpses at the figure lying so still on the gurney. He, too, was a very large, black-haired man. Both men's features were obscured by the windows and the movement

9

of the vehicle, but Leonie thought she caught a resemblance. Were they brothers?

The man turned and vivid blue eyes, unseeing, met hers for a fraction of a second. They seemed full of despair.

Poor man, thought Leonie, then turned her thoughts to her own problems and the uncertainty of her future.

★   ★   ★

FBI agent Christopher Culhane shut his mind to the excited babble of the crowd, the hysterical keening of the siren, and the frantic but controlled activity of the ambulance crew around him. His unfocused eyes held no more of an image of Leonie than they did the rest of his surroundings. He felt a despairing certainty that the man lying so still and bloodless before him would no longer be alive by the time they reached the hospital.

Culhane's mind reached and probed every corner of his memory of those brief moments from the time he had reached Tom Callahan's side until the victim slipped into unconsciousness, murmuring just one word.

'Tape!' Callahan had whispered urgently, his glazing eyes plainly mistaking Culhane for someone else. And there had been a tape, ostensibly a musical selection for the tape deck of the car now lying bloodstained and abandoned. If it turned out to be just what it

10

seemed, he'd be no wiser.

Was it all to be in vain—that wild ride from the mountain cabin back to the city and the tiresome hours of surveillance here? How was he supposed to save a marked man's life without some information? If there was nothing on the tape and Callahan died without speaking further, then Judge John Warwick was doomed.

He concentrated all his mental powers on the blood-drained face before him. Live! Live! he begged silently of the man who, superficially at least, looked so much like himself.

He did not dream that the beautiful auburn-haired woman who followed his passing with pitying eyes would soon be caught up with him in a drama of violence, vengeance and murder.

CHAPTER TWO

INVESTIGATE...
to follow a track, to search.

As the ambulance lurched through the crowded city streets, shrieking and yelping, Christopher Culhane reflected upon the swiftness of the events that had brought him from a tranquil mountaintop to his present

11

situation. He was no stranger to action and violence, but even he was somewhat disoriented by the abrupt change of scene. Mostly because it had been so completely unexpected.

He had intended a brief stop in town to see his old friend, Jimmy Mosely, before backpacking into his favorite mountains. And here he was, back at work on what should have been the first day of his vacation. He shook his head wonderingly, considering the strange turn of events. It had all happened so fast it seemed unreal.

He had been kidding Jimmy about his job. 'You're much better looking than any sheriff I've ever seen on TV. You'd better ease down south a bit and let Hollywood look you over, instead of wasting your talents like this. Nothing ever happens here.'

'Take your own advice,' Jimmy had retorted. 'You were always the glamour boy of the Academy. But seriously, Chris, I like it here. The pay's not much, to be sure, but the livin' sure is easier, and with Barbara gone now...' He left the sentence dangling, his face twisting with pain, then finished lamely, 'You know.'

'Yes, he did know. His own loss was still keenly felt.

'Say, do you ever hear from...?' he had begun brightly, trying to change the subject quickly, when the clamor of the telephone cut across the banal question.

'Sheriff's office. Mosely.' Jim held up a be-with-you-in-a-minute hand. Suddenly he stiffened, and his face came alive. 'Hold on.' His eyes were bright with excitement as he grabbed paper and pencil. He scribbled furiously, then nodded to the unseen caller. 'Got it. We'll be right up there.' His half-smile toward Culhane was rueful, a little grim. 'Nothing happens here, eh? Somebody saw a plane go down back of Thompson's Ridge—one of the remotest areas. Explosion. Fire. The whole bit. Probably no survivors, but we'll have to go see. Sorry to cut your visit short, Chris. Unless...' He stopped, reluctant to ask, but Chris grinned, understanding the unfinished appeal.

'I know. You could use some help. Why not? I can...' He broke off as the door sprang back to admit an agitated boy of about fifteen. White-faced and breathless, he practically fell into the room in a series of awkward maneuvers—the combination of too-large feet and seemingly unconnected joints that only a gangling adolescent can achieve.

Mosely, intent on his preparations, did not look around, for apparently the sounds were familiar. 'Hey, Richard! You almost missed me. Gotta run, but I do want you to meet an old friend and partner-in-crime.' He waved a hand behind his back. 'This is Chris

13

Culhane.'

The boy did not respond, and Mosely, his mind on the phone call, only now registered that fact and turned to note his son's disheveled appearance. His expression turned to alarm. 'Dick! What happened? What's wrong?'

The boy stood as if rooted, pale-faced and wide-eyed, his eyes fixed with strange intensity on Culhane's face. He took a careful inventory of the height and breadth of the older man, with his thickly curling black hair, his piercing blue eyes, then drew a ragged breath and threw his father an anguished look. 'Your friend?' he croaked in dismay. 'Dad! This is the man who just shot at me!'

Jim Mosely pulled up as abruptly as an animal lassoed in a calf-rope. 'What are you saying? Chris goes back to the Academy days at Quantico with me. He's still with the FBI.'

The boy looked confused and more stricken than ever. His father, frowning, surveyed his torn and dirty clothing, the cuts and scratches that covered his arms. 'Say! I didn't hear . . . Where's Sultan? Did you walk in? Where's the horse?'

'Whoa, Jimmy, back up a minute!' Chris Culhane quietly cut off the distraught father's rapid-fire questions and eased the boy into a chair just in time. The youngster's knees jacknifed as if a string had been pulled, and he began to tremble.

'He really ought to lie down,' Chris muttered to Mosely. 'Whatever's happened he's had quite a shock.'

'Okay, son, take it easy now.' Mosely was back in control. 'It's okay. You're all right, and that's the main thing. You say someone shot at you? Who? And why?'

'I don't know, Dad.' Dick was having trouble keeping his voice steady, and his fists clenched and unclenched as he tried to keep from breaking down completely. 'Sultan threw a shoe, and I decided we'd both be better off if I led him down the old road leading to Sander's shack. Nobody's ever lived there that I can remember. But when I came close there was a man just getting out of a red jeep. I was so surprised I stopped short, and I couldn't even move when he jerked out a gun and fired at me. It was so unexpected I just froze. He missed, of course. Probably fired too fast because I took him by surprise too. Sultan spooked and ran off, and then I jumped for cover and took off myself, but not before I got a good look at him. And Dad, I swear, he looked just like Mr. Culhane here. At least from that distance.'

As Mosely turned to Chris and caught the expression on his face his eyes widened in astonishment. 'You know who he is, Chris?'

'I'm not sure,' Culhane said slowly. 'I do know someone who looks that much like me generally, and oddly enough he's connected

15

with a case I just finished. But he'd have no interest in me personally. I can't imagine what he'd be doing away up here anyway.

'You remember the Petrosino affair, Jim? That was the case, and it was a sizzler. But that's over now—evidence, trial, sentencing, the whole thing. And Petrosino is finally behind bars. After all these years, John Warwick was the first judge to make an indictment stick by sentencing that slimy character. You remember?'

'Sure,' Mosely said. 'Alfredo Petrosino, kingpin of the underworld, finally brought to justice. Kept all the newspapers in the black for months. But who is that guy up there?' He stopped, struck by a sudden thought. 'You think there might be a connection between that plane crash and this character?'

'That's exactly what I'm wondering,' Culhane said thoughtfully. 'But I can't imagine what...' He broke off. 'Make a quick phone call for me, will you? I want to check something out with the office.'

Mosely made his connection and handed the receiver to Chris without comment, then waited patiently for the brief conversation to end.

There was controlled excitement in Culhane's brilliant blue eyes as he turned back to the sheriff. 'So! Petrosino has flown the coop. A very cleverly engineered jailbreak. Which means the man up at that

16

cabin just might be Tom Callahan, Petrosino's right-hand man and heir apparent. In which case he's not up there to admire the scenery. He does look enough like me to make Dick jump to the wrong conclusion.' He turned to smile at the boy before continuing. 'He's number one next to Petrosino, and was supposed to take over when the old man retired. Tell me, Dick, was he coming or going? Could you tell?'

'Oh, sure.' The boy's voice was much stronger. 'He was coming in. He had just pulled up in the clearing around the cabin and was getting out of the red jeep. That's when he saw me coming through the trees.'

His father joined in. 'Did you see or hear anything of a light plane going down? It must have been right in that area.'

'No, Dad, I didn't see or hear a thing. But you know how that can be. If I was on the wrong side of the mountain or the wind wasn't right I'd miss it.' Some of the boy's color had returned and he looked much better. 'Where did it happen?'

'Just the other side of Thompson's Ridge. They're checking flight plans involving routes over this area now. They said . . .' He broke off to exclaim, 'What is it, Chris? You look like a comic strip character with a light bulb turned on over his head.'

'I did get a thought,' Culhane said dryly, his lips pursed in concentration, 'but it

17

doesn't jibe with filing flight plans. Let's see
... Dick, how long did it take you to get
down here to the office?'

'Oh, about two, two-and-a-half hours,' the
boy said. 'On foot, of course. It wouldn't take
too long in a vehicle. Why?'

'Well, it's wild, but if what I'm thinking is
true, it would explain a lot of things. Tell you
what, Jim.' He turned to his friend. 'If it's
okay with you, I'd like to go up and check out
that cabin while you investigate your plane
crash. They're probably gone by now, but if
I'm right...' He stopped and shook his head
in bemusement. 'I know it's crazy, but if I'm
right...' He trailed off again.

Mosely eyed the FBI man with eyebrows
quirked as he gathered up the last of his
equipment. '"They"?'

'I won't tell you just yet, Jim. The idea's
too far out. They'd lock me up in a rubber
room if it didn't materialize.' He threw
Mosely a quick grin, then sobered
immediately. 'But I can tell you this. If, by
some wild chance I have figured right, we've
opened up a whole new can of worms.'

'You really have me mystified now,' Jim
complained, 'but if you don't want to pursue
it further...' He shrugged, leaving it at that.

'I really don't, Jim,' Culhane said quietly.
'Not at the moment. But I'll need your help.'

'Me? How?'

'I want you to look for something while

18

you're combing that Thompson Ridge area for the plane.'

'Such as?' Jim asked. 'I do need to check out the plane crash, but I want to know who's been shooting at my son, and why?'

'Why don't you let me handle that angle, Jim? They're almost certainly gone by now, but I can give that cabin a good going-over while you do what's required of you. Just keep your eye out for something stuffed under a rock, into the brush, something like that.'

'Like what?' Mosely asked.

Culhane didn't answer immediately. 'Don't worry about me if I'm not back before dark,' he said, preoccupied. 'I'd better not go all the way in the vehicle. Best to stay out of sight. I'll check back with you later.' Then, seeing Mosely's lips part with a look of exasperation, he held up a quickly placating hand. 'Don't shoot, Sheriff, I'll talk!' he teased briefly, then answered the question directly. 'What I want you to look for is...' His dramatic pause was quite unconscious. 'A parachute!'

★   ★   ★

Some time later he watched from his hiding place as the red jeep, surprisingly still there, careened down the rough track close enough for him to identify the driver. Tom Callahan, without a doubt. Alone.

19

And where was the Big Man himself? The question had plagued Chris as he wound his way down the mountain back to his van. Technically, he could have said, 'So, what?' But it never occurred to him to do anything but postpone his vacation to unravel the mystery.

For a brief time he thought he had done just that. Tom Callahan's presence far afield, he reasoned, was explained by Petrosino's disappearance after the jailbreak. That was exactly wily old Alfredo's style. A fake airplane crash. Or, to be more accurate, a real crash but a fake death, a prearranged explosion ensuring that the real death, that of his private pilot, would leave no witness.

For a while it all seemed to fall into place. He had it all figured out. Petrosino, secretly picked up by Callahan after he parachuted to safety, hidden in the back of the jeep, now free to enjoy his retirement and his ill gotten gains under a new identity.

Only it hadn't worked out that way. True, later investigation would show the plane to be rigged for timed explosives. And Petrosino, in spite of his age, was as capable of parachuting to safety as he was of sacrificing his own pilot. Not only was he a fitness 'nut,' in superb condition, but he had been a paratrooper during World War II, serving with the famed 82nd Airborne. His jumping skills were kept honed at a sky diving club. His money, his power, and his underworld connections could easily assure him a new identity, complete with beautifully forged documents of all kinds.

So far, so good. Great detective work. Three cheers for Christopher Culhane. Except that all of it was shot down when Chris again made contact with Jimmy Mosely.

The sheriff and his deputy had found the site of the crash well before dark. The force of the explosion hadn't left much to identify, but it had been established beyond a doubt that the plane was indeed Petrosino's. What blew Culhane's theory completely was the fact that there was indisputable evidence of *two* bodies found in the wreckage of the plane.

'And I thought I had it all figured out,' Chris complained. 'Petrosino breaks out of jail, secretly stows a parachute in his plane, pulls a gun on his pilot from the back seat, somewhere near the mountain meadow, then jumps, having previously arranged for the plane to blow up. Callahan picks him up at the cabin, and off he goes with a new ID and a bag full of money, never to be seen again. Callahan takes over the organization, as he was supposed to when Petrosino retired. The old man—who wasn't that old, by the way—always said he would bow out while he was still in good enough shape to enjoy life. He would have been even more motivated by the

21

fact that he faced spending the rest of his life in jail.'

'And Callahan, only too happy to take over, keeps the deep, dark secret,' suggested Mosely.

'He was always Petrosino's favorite. In fact, lived with him. The rest of the gang resented the special treatment he always got. What they didn't know was that the old man had legally adopted Callahan when he was just a kid he'd picked up off the streets. Apparently he saw some promise in the boy, gave him an Ivy League education and groomed him to be the son and heir he never had. He let the boy keep his own name to hide the fact. I figured the time had come now for Callahan's takeover, with Petrosino destined to spend the rest of his days behind bars. Yeah. I had it all figured out. Except.'

'Except,' Jim had agreed morosely, 'there are *two* corpses in the morgue.'

'Hey, wait a minute!' Something in Culhane's voice made Mosely straighten up alertly. '*We* know that, but Callahan couldn't have! Why did he leave before finding out what had happened to his boss, his own father? There's no way he could have gotten that news before he left the cabin. There was no means of communication there. Just a tape player.'

'You're right,' Jim agreed. 'According to what you told me, he was already heading out of the area before we returned. How could he have known?'

'I think,' Culhane said thoughtfully, 'I'll just postpone my vacation a little longer. I'd like to know just what Mr. Tom Callahan is up to.'

CHAPTER THREE

ANTICIPATE...
to look forward: to expect.

The two men stood at the rail of the departing cruise ship, conspicuously quiet amidst all the commotion. They were not there on pleasure and each was lost in his own disquieting thoughts. Both were big men, powerfully built, one very dark, the other fair. They stood apart, as yet unknown to one another, oblivious to the interest in their contrasting good looks.

A milling, supercharged crowd bent on adventure and excitement surged around them, glancing curiously at the pair. It was a rare sight to see such striking-looking men apparently traveling alone. Tall, commanding in appearance, they stood out like islands in an open sea.

Sanna Warwick stole a look at her daughter's bright, drooping head and groaned inwardly. Here was a beautiful young woman not even noticing two uncommonly handsome young men!

She felt a stab of pain as a sudden vivid image flashed into her mind: Leonie on her wedding day, so lovely it almost hurt to look at her. Her skin and eyes had glowed as if lighted from within.

Then the bride's amber-flecked green gaze slid from under lush lashes to assess her mother. 'Beautiful! Perfectly beautiful!' Her voice had choked as she tried to laugh. 'I think I'll ask you to wait outside, Madam. I don't want you upstaging the bride!' Then her chin had quivered, her voice quavered and she wailed, 'Oh, Mother!' in the same tone she had used to show Sanna bruises and skinned knees. Total desolation.

'Hey!' Sanna had protested, trying to get control of her own rampant emotions. 'You're not leaving forever. We'll be close enough to keep in touch. And listen, young lady, you are not about to cry over all that expensive makeup!' They had managed to laugh then, but both of them knew that things would never be quite the same again.

Looking back now, Sanna considered that neither of them could foresee just how drastic the change would be. Her throat tightened as she compared Leonie now with that vivid bride. The beauty was still there. The glow had been completely extinguished. A few short months ago. An eternity ago.

Sanna's eyes suddenly stung with unshed tears. It was only with difficulty that she contained them as they went down to their cabins.

As they looked around the spare and compact quarters that would be Leonie's home for the next two weeks, Sanna said with a false gaiety, 'Imagine! We're actually on a cruise ship. I still can't believe it. It's something I've always wanted to do.'

Her husband looked at her in mild astonishment and said, 'You should have been more vocal about it. You'd mentioned a cruise a time or two, but you never said much when we planned all those trips.'

'You mean *you* planned them, dear.' Sanna smiled fondly at him, her eyes crinkling in amusement, in spite of the tartness of her tone. 'And I enjoyed every one of them—thoroughly. But I knew how much your choices meant to you, and they were fine with me. But I'm glad we finally did get here.' She and the judge exchanged looks of complete understanding.

That's how it should be, Leonie thought with a pang. In a good marriage each one cares about what's important to the other.

She knew they had had problems over the years, as did all couples living in an intimate relationship. And she knew that the end result she was now observing was something like the seemingly effortless performance of a superb athlete who shows only the expertise, not the agony that earned it. But somehow she had always assumed she'd be as blessed as her parents, that her own marriage would be as satisfactory as theirs. She couldn't have been more mistaken.

'A penny for your thoughts, Lee,' John Warwick said, in the tone he used to use to tease her out of a bad humor when she was a child. Her mother, divining her thoughts, threw out a diversion before Leonie could answer.

'Oh, John, don't call her that. You know I don't like it. 'Leonie' is such a pretty name.'

'I agree,' Judge Warwick said amiably, 'but we all call you "Sanna" and I think "Suzanna" is a lovely name.'

'*Touché*,' Sanna laughed. 'But must you always be so reasonable? Just because you're a federal judge doesn't mean you're always right!'

They all laughed then, and Leonie was surprised to find herself joining in. She suddenly realized it was her first real laugh in many months. Her mother's lovely face had lit up so magically at the sound that she felt a stab of guilt. How pathetically grateful Sanna was to see even a glimpse of her daughter's former self. I'll make it up to her, Leonie thought, to both of them. They've suffered quite enough for my mistakes. I'm going to come off this cruise a different person, and we're going to start a whole new ball game.

Impulsively, she jumped up and kissed her mother warmly. 'You two are something else. Come on!' She took an arm of each and urged, 'Let's go up to the Promenade Deck and see what's going on. We have plenty of time before the dining room closes at nine. Dinner is buffet style this first night, with open seating, instead of the usual arrangement.'

'How do you know that?' Sanna asked.

Leonie looked surprised. 'Didn't you read the information in your folder? They can't seat everybody at once, so they usually have two seatings. But of course that's not practical for the first night. I thought you knew.'

Sanna flushed, suffusing the fine fair skin that was so like Leonie's. 'Well, actually I didn't take time to look at the folder. I thought there would be plenty of time to educate myself on all aspects of the trip once we got aboard.'

'Well, of course you can,' Leonie said tactfully, feeling another pang of remorse. She knew that ordinarily her mother would have read and remembered everything in anticipation of the trip. In fact, knowing Sanna as she did, she would even expect her to spend a good deal of time researching all the places they would visit. Because of the misery of these past months, Sanna could probably think of nothing but running away from the whole sorry mess of her daughter's ruined marriage.

Leonie remembered only nodding apathetically in answer to her parents' persuasive arguments that she needed to 'get away.' She had said nothing, but let them run in their too-bright tones of staged enthusiasm. Nothing had mattered at that point. Now she felt a fierce determination to shake off the unhappy past completely and make a fresh start. 'Come on!' she said again. 'I'm ready for action!' She wore her old grin as she added, 'But we'll have to get out of here. There's no room to swing. This cabin is barely big enough for me, let alone all of us. I hope you two don't have to go in and out of yours sideways!' She felt almost lighthearted as they stepped out into the narrow passageway, and her spirits soared as she caught her parents exchanging looks of pure joy. Daddy was right—as usual. 'That clean sea air will clear the bad taste out of all our mouths,' he had declared.

'Let's not take the elevator,' Leonie said. 'Are you game for all those stairs? We're three decks down, you know.'

'Suits me,' said the judge. 'We've done nothing but sit and eat all day. I'll be glad of the exercise.'

'So will I,' Leonie said. 'From what I hear of these cruise ship meals, I may go home a candidate for Weight Watchers!'

'That'll be the day!' her father snorted, quite unlike his usual dignified self. 'Not with that prize-winning figure.' He grinned at her impishly, looking nothing like the imposing figure that commanded such respect on the judge's bench, then reached for his wallet. 'And I've got the pictures to prove it!'

They had nearly reached the end of the corridor, and Leonie and Sanna exchanged puzzled glances as he pulled some newspaper clippings out with a flourish. 'Ta-da! The fairest of them all.'

Sanna gave her husband an indulgent look, while Leonie cried out in horror. 'Daddy, you didn't! You brought that old stuff *along*? You're as bad as Doc Sanderson and the pictures of his grandkids. You are *not* going to show that thing around this ship!' She snatched at the papers he held. The judge, teasing, held them well out of reach. As tall as Leonie was, he was taller. He edged out of the narrow corridor into the open area of the stairwell, taunting her.

Leonie, flushed and laughing, made a desperate lunge in his direction. He sidestepped, and she fell straight into the arms of a man who was just turning into the passageway. It was the huge blond man she had seen on deck when they first arrived. His face held an expression that baffled her.

There followed the usual comic little dance

29

that results when two people get in each other's way, but finally the big man had the statuesque redhead firmly balanced on her own feet. They exchanged apologies, then went their separate ways. During the whole exchange his eyes had never left Leonie's face.

'I'm sorry, honey,' the judge apologized when they were alone again. Still, he didn't sound the least repentant as he added, 'But you have to admit that was a *very* good-looking young man. And apparently his cabin is on this deck too.'

'John!' his wife said in a very wifely tone. There was warning as well as reproof in her look.

But Leonie smiled fondly at her irrepressible father. 'Oh, it's all right, Mom,' she said easily. 'You know Dad's an incurable romantic. And I don't suppose I'll go the rest of my life avoiding men. It is ironic though. I'm probably the only female on board who isn't susceptible, and the first night out I meet one of the few unattached young men on the ship.'

So she *did* notice, Sanna thought, and the thought cheered her.

'You may not be susceptible,' the judge chuckled, 'but he certainly was. Did you see the look on his face? He was absolutely zapped.'

'That's good for the old ego,' Leonie said

30

in a bright, artificial tone, but her pulses were pounding, remembering the bulge of muscle and the intimidating hardness of the massive chest into which she had blundered. Tiny shivers pricked her spine, a conditioned response to a man's touch.

Something caught her eye. Glad of a diversion, she stopped to pick it up off the floor. 'Here.' She held out her hand to her father. 'With all those goings-on you lost your precious clipping.'

The judge stared at her in surprise and shook his head. 'No, I didn't, honey. Look.' He held out his own hand, displaying the newspaper article. 'What do you have there?'

'I don't believe this,' Leonie said. 'It's the same thing.'

'Can't be,' her father declared flatly.

In answer Leonie opened out the clipping fully and read: '"On the left, Judge John F. Warwick, with his daughter, Leonie," etcetera.'

'But, where in the world . . .?' Sanna began.

Leonie, recalling the moment of impact with the blond giant, said slowly, 'It was his—Big Boy's. He must have had it in his hand when we collided. I can't imagine why.'

An old newspaper picture and a man's face changing color on suddenly meeting that face in the flesh. Her forehead wrinkled. What could it mean? Oh, well, it didn't matter. A cruise ship was no place for a mystery.

31

She had not the faintest premonition of how that encounter would change her future, suddenly and dramatically, in the days to follow.

CHAPTER FOUR

CALCULATE...
to purpose or intend; to be selfishly and coldly scheming.

The big blond man strode rapidly down the Promenade Deck to a secluded corner offering a bank of empty deck chairs. He knew they'd be filling up soon. More than an hour had passed while he circulated freely without anyone making the expected contact.

He wasn't concerned. Callahan would show, sooner or later. There was nowhere to go and all the time in the world to wait. For once he agreed with Petrosino. It sure made things easier when the action was confined to a ship. No cops getting in the way either. At least, not any time soon. Not that cops ever cramped his style. They simply complicated things.

Petrosino had made much of trusting someone besides Callahan with the knowledge that he was still alive. 'Not even my own boys, Heinsohn! My own organization. Well,

Tom Callahan, but he's my right-hand man, of course. But nobody else.

'He'll give you the second half of your payment before you leave the ship and get the money to me when you've both finished. No personal contact on this job. I'm out of sight from now on. New name, new face. I can't call Tom; they'll be expecting that. He'll get his orders another way.

'Now listen, Heinsohn. I like your style, and your reputation. You done good work for me in the past. This is my biggest job—and the last. Couldn't trust nobody else with it. But it'll be a little tricky. Here's what you do.' And the instructions had followed.

Heinsohn reviewed some of them now. 'He'll have the same identification you do,' Petrosino had said on the phone. Now what the hell did that mean? He had nothing with which to identify himself in a special way. The idea of working with a partner rankled anyway. Even if they did have different assignments. He'd always been a loner. Oh well, he shrugged mentally. It really didn't matter. He was planning on rearranging some of Mr. Petrosino's arrangements anyway.

'You don't understand, Heinsohn,' Petrosino had explained when he'd remonstrated. 'I know you usually work alone, but there's a beautiful girl involved in this and well, Tom's the best but you can't trust him around women. I don't want anything interfering or distracting on this job. Besides, using two of you will help confuse the opposition.'

Heinsohn had wondered idly where Petrosino could be hiding out after breaking out of jail, but he wasn't really interested. It did amuse him to think what the Feds would give to have that information. They'd been coming out of the woodwork since Petrosino fell out of sight, knowing Judge Warwick to be in danger.

'I want to put the heat on Warwick every way I can,' Petrosino had continued. 'He'll do anything for that girl of his. Especially now, after what they been through with her divorce. Once he coughs up, you can let her go. I got nothing against her. But the old man goes, after I make him sweat for that much money.

Petrosino had spat for emphasis. The sound was clear even over the telephone. 'Stupid old bastard! Everybody else was reasonable. That's what I got them high-priced lawyers for. This boy wouldn't play. I know he's got plenty of money, what with his real estate and oil interests, but nobody can rake up a cool million in cash without sweating some.

'We'll fix 'em. Scare the hell out of him with his daughter kidnapped, then hit him in the wallet. If he'd been smart he'd 'a' made money, like the rest of them, not lost it. Well, he missed his chance. You snatch the girl, Callahan takes care of him, and we're even. I retire happy to enjoy the mountain air.

'Everybody thinks I packed it in when my plane crashed. Of course I lost a good pilot, but what the hell, he knew he was in a dangerous business.' Heinsohn could imagine the other man's careless shrug, the lipless mouth widening. 'And they'll never find that parachute in those mountains. Me and Callahan made it out nice as you please. There he was, Johnny-on-the-spot with the jeep. Good boy, Callahan. He'll do a good job in my place when he takes over. You ain't never met him yet, have ya?'

No, Heinsohn thought now, mocking the bad grammar, I ain't never met him yet. But that's okay too. I need time to think things out. He slipped a paperback out of his pocket. He'd been this route before, traveling alone as much as he did, and had no desire for conversation or casual alliances, especially with lonely women.

He thought about Donna. Could he expect a girl like that to be waiting for him when he got back? He worried about that every time he was gone. He'd been able to give her the furs and jewels she craved, but knew she got plenty of male attention the minute he was out of sight. This had to be his last trip! He'd made enough now for both of them to live like royalty the rest of their lives. He'd marry

35

her when this was over. That would really stake his claim and then he'd allow her no excuse for straying.

Under cover of the small book he reviewed his present situation. The Warwicks were here all right. No last-minute change of plans there. But he'd never expected to meet the girl face to face so soon. That had shaken him. What a beauty! He'd never had an assignment involving a woman before. And it was much easier to stick to business and forget about people as people when you'd never met them. But that newspaper photo didn't half do her justice. In the pink-and-white flesh, a green-eyed, auburn-haired beauty with her face and figure would shake up any man!

What a joke on him to bump into her, literally, almost immediately after he boarded. He laughed inwardly to think of the elaborate schemes he had concocted to arrange a meeting that looked casual. You couldn't get much more casual then nearly knocking a girl down! That had put him way ahead of the game. It would be quite natural because of it for him to try to see her again. What he needed now was a game plan.

'Play it by ear, Heinsohn.' He could almost hear the whiskey-roughened voice that always sounded as though Petrosino had gargled with bits of sandpaper. 'This ain't the same as chasin' people around city streets. But you're a pro; you'll know what to do. One good thing about it...' He had stopped long enough to give the characteristic hiccuping snort that passed for laughter. 'They ain't goin' nowhere, them Warwicks. It'd be a long swim and a cold one.'

He snorted again, then continued, 'How you do it, you and Callahan, is your own business. I don't care what either of you does just so's you snatch the girl and Callahan wastes the old man, not the other way around.' His gravel voice had grown sly and suggestive. 'I'm givin' ya the plum, boy. She's a real looker. When that Callahan gets a good look at her he'll be mad as hell that he didn't get your job. In fact he already is, just from that newspaper picture.' The old man had snorted then until he wheezed.

Heinsohn, reliving the scene, grimaced in distaste. Petrosino was always making crude remarks about women, trying to question him in intimate detail about his personal life. There was no way he'd believe that a big, good-looking dude who attracted women like a magnet could be anything but a fulltime stud.

Let Petrosino play his little game, think what he liked. He couldn't care less as long as the old man kept playing perfectly into his hands. This was his last assignment—he'd promised Donna that—and should be his crowning achievement. It gave him a grim satisfaction to think that if everything went as planned, Petrosino would soon be behind bars again, while he would go back to Donna a rich man.

It had taken a lot of time, hard work and careful planning to win Petrosino's confidence. It was just a happy coincidence that the syndicate leader had so many enemies he wanted to eliminate, and that he, Werner Heinsohn, was the supreme eliminator. That made it easier for him to pursue his own personal vendetta while taking Petrosino's money.

Heinsohn stopped his musing and came alert immediately. A tall dark man, almost as big as he was, had deliberately taken the chair next to his, although there were still many empty. Heinsohn looked him over. Good-looking guy, with that black, black hair and cobalt-blue eyes. Irish as Paddy's pig. Callahan? He waited.

The dark-haired man smiled and nodded, drew a clipping from his jacket pocket, then glanced briefly to see Heinsohn's reaction. 'Callahan?' Heinsohn questioned aloud without lowering his book. So this was Petrosino's 'identification.' Childish!

The other man nodded imperceptibly and Heinsohn said, 'I had one to match, but I lost it somewhere.' He didn't even bother to look at the clipping. 'No problem,' he went on, seeing the other's frown. 'It has to be me—an ordinary tourist couldn't possibly know your name or what was going on.'

The two men took each other's measure professionally, almost clinically, and quite openly.

The Irishman saw a man who was even bigger than he was, a Norse Viking of a man whose massive column of a neck met shoulders so broad and hard-muscled they seemed to be made of granite rather than flesh. His blond hair fell helter-skelter over his outsized but rather flat-topped head, all of it seeming to grow out of the same spot on the crown. It was fair as corn silk, and so fine it seemed almost fluid. Modishly long, it kept sliding into his pale eyes, but he seemed totally unaware of it except to shake it back with an impatient gesture. A small flame flickering in the back of his expressionless eyes hinted to the Irishman of some unidentifiable commitment, even fanaticism. Concerning what, he couldn't imagine.

Heinsohn, in turn, tried to match the things he had heard against the man sitting quietly next to him. His colorless eyes assessed a man most people would have described as 'big and brawny.' He had expected size and obvious strength. What was unexpected, and more impressive than the man's physical attributes, was an electric quality of sheathed control, conveying unmistakable domination of mind and emotions as well as muscle. There was an air of cool calculation about him that hinted at ruthlessless when necessary. More than an impressive man. A formidable one. Heinsohn quickly revised his expectation of meeting a brash loudmouth, quick to brag about his prowess with girls and guns. Perhaps he only displayed his aggressive masculinity in the presence of women. Just as well. If he was going to be forced to work with this Irishman he had every right to expect complete professionalism.

Without realizing it he turned on the black-haired man a look that would have completely intimidated most people. It did not occur to him that the other man's face was carefully devoid of expression.

The Irishman recognized that flat look of emptiness in Heinsohn's pale eyes. He had seen it before. It declared that the taking of another human's life would be, for the blond giant, a completely impersonal thing.

CHAPTER FIVE

COORDINATE...
to work together in a common action or effort.

The two men's wary evaluation of each other broke off as Heinsohn gestured toward a couple of people coming toward them. 'That orientation meeting must be over. You know, where we were supposed to meet the crew, cruise personnel and all that. I figured we had more important introductions to make.' He looked knowingly at the Irishman, who simply nodded, then he continued. 'There'll be more coming out now and this place will really be jammed. Let's put on our act here, and then we'll move into the lounge. The band will be starting up soon and we can talk better there.' Heinsohn's tourist mask fell into place as he held out his hand. 'Werner Heinsohn here, from Des Moines.'

The other man broke out in a brilliant smile and said, as they shook hands. 'Hello. Tom Callahan, from St. Louis. Most people just call me "Irish."' His fine voice was deep and resonant.

Heinsohn smiled easily, keeping up the charade. 'We may be the only Midwesterners among all these Texans and Californians.'

'You're right,' Irish laughed, displaying most of his magnificent teeth again. 'Every other person I've met so far has been either one or the other.' He lifted his bulk smoothly and effortlessly, getting to his feet in one lithe movement, like a giant cat. 'Let's talk over a drink. First one's on me.'

Typical Irishman! thought Heinsohn. Can't talk without a drink in his hand. He wouldn't mind a drink now himself, but that

41

was one thing he was very careful about when on a job. He wasn't too hopeful that the Irishman felt the same way. What he'd heard of Callahan's reputation was the classical wine-women-and-song routine. But he answered easily enough. 'Sounds like a good idea.'

As they wormed their way along the now-crowded Promenade Deck, Heinsohn decided he'd have as little to do with Callahan as possible, except as they had to coordinate their assignments. He knew the Irishman was a very capable man—he'd have to be to have the position he held with the organization. Not only Petrosino's right-hand man, but the one who would take over when Petrosino stepped out of the picture. Which meant after they'd finished here. Well, that might be all well and good for Callahan, but no organization for him, thank you. Free-lance all the way.

Heinsohn watched the man moving in front of him. The beautifully-muscled body, big as it was, wove lightly, almost gracefully, through the thickening crowd. I'll bet that one cuts a wide swathe with the women, he thought. Quite the lady-killer. And, from what Petrosino said, quick to tell you about it. Yet there was no denying the almost tangible aura the man had of competency, cool efficiency, perfect self-control. Well, we all have our weaknesses. As long as the

Irishman did not mix business with pleasure...

Once inside, the two men found a small table in the lounge, close to the band. 'Perfect,' Irish said. 'You hold the fort while I get the ammunition.'

He was back shortly, a glass in each hand. 'Guess what?' The dark man's grin was almost a leer. 'There's a beautiful redhead in here we both want to meet. Do we just waltz up and ask her to dance?'

'Is she alone?' Heinsohn asked abruptly, anxious to get down to business.

'No,' Irish answered. 'They're all here. But there's just one Warwick I'm really interested in.'

Heinsohn's eyes narrowed. 'I hope you're thinking of the right one,' he said caustically. 'It's the judge who's your business, not the girl.'

'You don't need to rub it in,' Irish said, with obvious resentment. 'I can't see why Mr. P. wouldn't let me handle that part of it.'

Well I know why, Heinsohn thought, trying not to show his distaste. He sighed inwardly. Bad enough to be saddled with a partner. But this one! If they were going to bring the job off he was going to have to keep this clown's mind above his belt and keep reminding him who had what assignment. But he only said placatingly, 'Maybe it's because I've had more experience with this kind of thing, and he knows how good you are at the other. Mr. P. said we might get our heads together to figure out the time and place for you to do your thing.'

Irish glared at him. 'I can tell you right now, mister, I won't need any help.' His chin lifted in an arrogant gesture. 'I can handle that without any interference from you. Let's get that straight!' Then his quick flare of anger seemed to evaporate as quickly as it had come and his engaging grin returned. 'How about you? Sure you don't need any help with that babe?'

Heinsohn's nostrils flared as he surveyed his uncouth companion, but he spoke mildly enough, his voice rising to counteract the noise of the band which had just struck up a tune from the forties. 'Mr. P. thought it safer to split the assignments, as you know. Not only will it be easier that way, but it may well help to confuse the opposition. After I bring the girl back and get the rest of my payment I'll fall out of sight and you'll have a clear field.'

'Okay. But listen, there's plenty of time for business. Let's just relax and have a good time tonight. We can't have that beautiful girl getting lonesome her first night on board.' The Irishman started to rise.

'Just a minute. Sit down!'

Heinsohn's voice seemed to stop Irish in midair. He sat down again but threw the other man an abrasive look.

'Don't you think you'd better keep away from the Warwicks a while?' Heinsohn asked. 'Not only is it my job to snatch the girl, but I've already met her.' He described the fortuitous encounter on A-deck.

'Boy, are you a fast worker!' Irish was admiring.

'No,' Heinsohn admitted, 'it was pure luck. But the point is it would be natural for me to use that as an excuse to see her again. We've got to get friendly if I'm to have any chance of getting her away from her family. I have an idea they stick pretty close.'

'But I've got to get friendly, too, if I'm to get an opportunity to waste the judge,' Irish protested. 'It will be easier to get closer to him if he trusts me.'

'Maybe so, but remember: the girl goes first. You don't do anything until after the ransom money is paid.'

'I know that!' Irish was disgusted. 'But you're going to have a lot of time alone with that girl, and I . . .'

Heinsohn cut him off. 'Listen. What you do with your private life is your own business. But I'm not going to let you do anything that will jeopardize *my* job. And let me tell you something else, Callahan.' Heinsohn was having trouble relaxing his jaw. 'I'm only talking to you now because Mr. P. said we should get together. But I want you to

45

stay out of my end of the business and leave the girl alone.'

He listened to himself in astonishment. What did he care about that girl? Then he realized it really wasn't that. There was just something about Callahan that got his guard up. The guy was trouble. Every instinct told him so. And he had lived this long and gotten this far because his instincts had been good.

He did not consider himself a fearless man. A man without fear was a fool. But in his work he had developed a fine-tuning of senses and extrasensory perceptions that produced a kind of constructive fear which had saved his life on many occasions. He felt this visceral apprehension now. Afraid of saying too much, he rose and strode away without a backward glance.

Irish, who had given him a mocking salute with his glass, looked after him thoughtfully. You just think you're the only one to get close to Leonie Warwick, he reflected. Go ahead; take the first dance or two. But I've got my campaign mapped out, too. I just need a little more time to work on strategy. What, for instance, do I tell her when she asks me what I do for a living? He smiled an oddly secretive smile, as if mocking himself. I know, he thought, I'll make it really good. I'll tell her I work for the FBI!

He gave an enigmatic shrug and set his still full glass down as he rose from the table. The small sardonic smile returned as he looked at the unfinished drink and muttered to Heinsohn's retreating back, 'I am probably ruining the reputation of good Irishmen everywhere.'

CHAPTER SIX

COMPLICATE...
to twist or twine together, making complex or involved.

A shower and change of clothing early next morning heightened Leonie's determination to break out of the murky fog that had stifled her for so long. Last night's activities in the company of the big blond man had been a good start. I'm different already, she told herself. And there'll be no more glooming around. What's done is done, and it's time I looked ahead.

She faced her reflection thoughtfully as she made up her face with care. It was a long time since she had taken such pains in getting dressed. Mom and Dad were right, she decided, remembering her parents' persuasive arguments to get away, following the sordid courtroom scenes of the divorce hearing. New places and new faces did make a difference. To her surprise, she found excitement rising like long-buried desire. She reached for the door, astonished at her eagerness to get on with a new life. The door would not open.

Only mildly annoyed at first, she turned and twisted until she realized that nothing was going to work. She'd never heard of a lock you couldn't open from the inside, but there it was. Now what? Oh well, there must be somebody out there who'd fetch a steward. There had been numbers of them scurrying around with their huge key rings when they'd boarded at Vancouver. She banged on the door. 'Hello! Is anybody out there? I'm locked in!'

There was no answer although she listened carefully. Where was everybody? She banged the door mightily in her frustration, then abruptly stopped, appalled at her lack of control. What's happened to me? she thought angrily, and turned away to plop disconsolately into the chair that served the combination desk and dresser. Her newfound enthusiasm seemed to drain away. You never used to be like this, she told herself bitterly, falling apart over every little thing.

She was sitting very still, fighting the familiar waves of despair that threatened to engulf her again, when a knock came at the door. Her head came up abruptly, pride pushing back the tears that were so close.

'Are you all right in there?' A deep voice, assured and reassuring. A beautiful voice.

48

Leonie immediately felt strangely steadied and strengthened, and her voice was composed as she answered. 'I'm fine, but something's wrong with the lock. I can't get out.'

A rumbling laugh. 'You're not the only one. I've already rescued two others. These locks are weird. Hold tight, and I'll find the steward again. We'll have you out of there in a jiffy.'

What a magical voice! She could imagine herself lost in the spell of a tropical night with those mellow tones whispering close. As his footsteps died away she felt her pulse quicken, and an undeniable warmth flooded her cheeks. I can't believe you! she told herself in disgust. After what you've been through, to react like this to an exciting male voice! Remember the last time you succumbed to all those macho charms and found that was all there was? You're supposed to be 'older and wiser' now. 'Once burned, twice shy' . . . she glared at herself in the mirror and muttered aloud, 'Any more clichés you need to remind you how stupid you were? And how dearly you paid for it?'

Returning footsteps cut short her self-reproach. There was a rattle of keys and the door opened on a slight but surprisingly tall young Oriental, all smiles and large teeth. 'I am Sam, your steward. Please to show you.' There followed a brief lesson in what to

49

push and what not to push so Leonie's problem would not be repeated, then he bowed and left, still smiling.

She hadn't been able to see past him into the dim passageway. Had her rescuer gone? Or had he never returned, simply directed the steward to the proper cabin?

And what do I care? She tossed her head defiantly, and glared once more at the lovely flushed face with the angry green eyes as she snatched up her purse from the dresser and left the room.

He was waiting discreetly at the end of the corridor. Somehow she was not surprised to recognize him as the second of the men they had first noticed as they came on board. This was the dark one, and everything matched the marvelous voice that had rumbled from the depths of his heavily-muscled chest. A strongly-chiseled, firm-jawed face and very direct eyes that were vividly blue under the heavy dark brows and black curly hair. One of those incredibly handsome Irishmen, if she ever saw one! She steeled herself, prepared to resist the good looks as well as the Irish charm and blarney she felt sure accompanied them. Fire away, Irish! she challenged him mentally. Here's one campaign that's going to fizzle before you ever start it!

But he merely gave her a polite impersonal smile and said, with the stilted good manners of a small boy who has been well coached,

'Glad to see you got out all right. Enjoy your day.' And off he went, without so much as a backward glance.

Leonie felt her face flush—that hateful wash of color that came so quickly and easily to fire her white skin. 'Well, Miss Conceit! Serves you right!' she muttered to herself. 'You deserve to be embarrassed. Beauty queen is ignored by handsome man who is supposed to react like every other man she's ever met. That'll l'arn ya, my girl!' She smiled ruefully and was still laughing at herself when she found her parents awaiting her on the Promenade Deck.

'How lovely you look in that pale green, Leonie,' her mother said as she surveyed the carefully made-up face and meticulously groomed hair. 'It matches your eyes perfectly. And I do believe you're more relaxed already.' Sanna's expression was expectant and just a little anxious.

Poor Mom, Leonie thought. She's afraid to be too hopeful. Has it been so long since I've looked and acted human? Impulsively she hugged the older woman. 'I feel fine. And I'm not usually the early bird you two are by inclination. What's on the schedule for today?'

Sanna fished a long piece of paper from her purse. 'Here's a little one-page newspaper they put out every evening to make announcements and give information on what's going on every day. Let's see.' Her bright head bent over the sheet. 'At nine there are lectures, one of them on Prince Rupert, which is our first stop. Or, if you feel athletic, they offer volleyball and ping-pong. After lunch, there's a movie that describes Juneau, our next stop, and the icecap flights. That's down in the theater. There are also choices of sketching and painting classes, or playing bridge. My first priority comes right after breakfast.' Sanna's eyes, bright and clear in spite of the early hour, danced merrily over her coffee as she challenged Leonie to guess.

'I give up,' Leonie played along.

'Well, you may not need it, my love, but I need all the help I can get. My first stop is the beauty shop, to make an appointment for this weekend.'

Leonie sniffed. 'Listen to the woman. I only hope I can look half as good when I'm your age.' Her eyes were warm with frank admiration as she looked at her lovely mother, still shapely, if a little plump, still vibrant. A few gray hairs amidst the copper glow, and the presence of tiny wrinkles in her sensitive skin did not detract in the least from her spectacular good looks. Leonie was quite sincere. She fervently hoped she had a chance of doing as well as her mother in maintaining her own attractiveness. There had been mornings when she was married to Walter when she'd looked in the mirror fully

52

expecting to see that her hair had turned white overnight. Now she quickly dismissed the harsh memories of the past and returned to the subject at hand.

'But don't we have plenty of time to make appointments in the beauty shop?' Leonie asked.

'Not really,' Sanna said. 'They recommend you do this the first day at sea. I checked and there are only two operators for all these females on board. Besides, the shop is only open while we're at sea, not when we stop in port.'

Leonie's luminous eyes widened in delight as she surveyed her mother. Sanna had certainly changed, too. Already she was more like the bubbly, exuberant Sanna of old, making jokes and keeping on top of everything. You'll see, she promised her mother silently. I'll be different, too. I'll be a new woman when we come off this cruise. Her voice was light-hearted as she answered. 'You're way ahead of me, Mom. We're going to give you back your old job.'

'My old job?' Sanna laughed, puzzled.

'Yep. As W.I.O.'

'As *what*?'

'Warwick Information Officer.' Leonie grinned mischievously, then laughed outright at her parents' expressions. Both were beaming at her as if she were a precocious three-year-old who had just said something clever. 'Know what?' she added, feeling like a giddy youngster. 'I'm famished! This sweet roll wasn't nearly enough. What time is breakfast? I'm ready to eat!'

The Warwicks stared as though she had made an astonishing announcement, and said in unison, 'You *are*?'

Again Leonie felt a pang of remorse. They've even been worrying about my lack of appetite, she reflected. I can't take away their hurt, but at least I can make a real effort to climb out of this hole I've been in for so long. 'I could eat a horse,' she declared, laughing.

'I doubt that's on the menu, dear,' her father said, displaying the comical look he wore when making one of his heavy-handed attempts at humor. 'And,' he continued, 'all this talk about food and beauty shops, and you left off the most important item of the day.'

'What's that?' Sanna demanded.

'There's a lifeboat drill at 3:00 P.M. and we are assigned to Lifeboat Station Number Eight. So there, you two. I've learned a thing or two myself!'

They laughed at the judge's expression in having upstaged his two females, and Leonie felt her spirits lift. Until now all she'd heard about time healing wounds had seemed to evaporate somewhere between head and heart. For the first time since her marriage had crumbled she felt a change was truly possible. By the time they reached the dining room, her face was aglow with expectation, and many a head turned to watch the exquisite auburn-haired girl with the model's face and figure.

Breakfast over, Leonie couldn't wait to get back to the Prom Deck, as they had learned to call it. She didn't want to miss any of that lovely landscape they were passing. They were fortunate in finding three inside deck chairs together, and Leonie slid into hers with a sigh of contentment. 'Isn't this beautiful?' she murmured. 'Where are we now, does anyone know?'

The judge waved a languid hand, feeling stuffed after an enormous breakfast. 'Ask your mother. I'm going to be very lazy. Imagine. No telephone, no interruptions, no court cases. Marvelous! Go away; I'm asleep!'

Leonie smiled at him. 'Go ahead and relax, Dad. You certainly need it. We'll leave you alone.' She turned to Sanna. 'Let's see your map please, Mom.'

Slender fingers traced their route thus far. 'Here you are,' Sanna said. 'We came out of Vancouver into Burrard Inlet, and when we passed under the Lion's Gate Bridge came into the Strait of Georgia.'

'Are we going through the Inside Passage now, then?' Leonie asked.

'Oh my, no. We don't get into that until some time tomorrow afternoon, after we leave

Prince Rupert. We only spend the morning there.'

'What are shopping possibilities on this trip—anything interesting?' Leonie asked.

'Oh, yes,' Sanna assured her. 'Of course, Alaskans have fabulous natural resources to use for their arts and crafts—ivory, jade, soapstone, and the famous gold nuggets as well as wood, furs, leather and other things. But they also make it easy to know just what you're buying. An article will bear one of two emblems. If it's the Silver Hand, it means it was handmade in Alaska by a native Alaskan—an Indian, Eskimo or Aleut artist or craftsman. If it bears the Alaska Resident emblem, that means it was handmade by an Alaskan who is not a native.'

'You really have been studying, Mom.' Leonie's green eyes softened as she looked at her mother.

Sanna, flushed with pleasure, looked suddenly younger and more animated than she'd been in months. 'Well,' she said, 'it's not everyone's cup of tea, but I've always wanted to read about the history and background of what I'm seeing and buying. It's not enough for me to simply pick up something that appeals to me. That way I feel as though I'm really taking home a bit of the place I visited.'

Seeing Sanna come alive again, Leonie and her now-attentive father kept silent, their alert looks encouraging her to continue. 'Did you know, for instance,' Sanna went on, 'that ivory can only be hunted by Eskimos? And soapstone sculpturing was developed during periods of ivory shortages?'

'More points for you, Mom,' Leonie laughed. 'I didn't know any of that. In fact, I'm not even sure of the source of their ivory. I thought ivory came from elephants.'

'It comes from walruses here, as a rule,' Sanna informed her. 'One of the things I particularly hope to find is a nice piece of scrimshaw I can afford.'

'That's what they call the etched pieces of ivory jewelry, isn't it?' Leonie asked.

'Yes, but it's not limited to jewelry. I've seen some beautiful examples in figurines and things like ship models. Of course, they cost the earth.'

'Speaking of expense,' Leonie asked, 'do you suppose I can find one of those hand-woven baskets that *I* can afford? Marianne Lindley was telling me about them before we left.'

'Good luck!' Sanna laughed. 'I understand the prices start at about $70, and that's for the smallest ones! Each one is unique. They're like snowflakes; no two designs are alike. And some of them are so tightly woven they'll hold water!'

'Really?' Leonie was amazed to find her interest in the trip so suddenly heightened.

All her old apathy was completely gone. 'I'm more impressed with you by the minute, Mother dear. I'm glad one of us cared enough to do some research.'

'I really enjoy it,' Sanna admitted. 'But I didn't do nearly as much in advance as I would have liked to.'

'No problem. I understand they have an excellent library aboard ship. You'll have plenty of time to get educated before we dock at each of our stops. By the way, what's to see in P.R.?'

'Don't be so disrespectful,' her mother laughed. 'P.R., as you so irreverently call it, is not only the most important port, but is also the center of industry of northern British Columbia. There's an excellent museum there, I'm told, and I'm anxious to see our first totem poles. By the way, if you want to shop at a Hudson's Bay store, Prince Rupert's the only place for us to do it. Once we get to Juneau we're out of Canada and in Alaska.'

'Well!' said Leonie admiringly. 'You really did your homework, Mom. I am impressed. You can just be our personal guide on this trip.'

'I'm just beginning,' Sanna warned her as she rose. 'Now that my breakfast is settled, I'm going to the lecture to learn more about what we'll see tomorrow. Want to come? No? Well, then, I'll meet you in the dining room for lunch. How about you, John?'

58

His answer was something between a grunt and a snore. She cocked a quizzical eye at her recumbent husband. 'Guess that answers my question,' she said wryly, waved a jaunty hand and was gone.

Leonie looked over at her father. How tired he looked. That Petrosino case had simply drained him. She would probably never know just what he'd been through; he didn't talk much about his work. But there had been a great deal of publicity because of Petrosino's notoriety, and she did know he was the first judge to bring sentence against this lord of the underworld. There had been hints that the failure of previous attempts was not due to lack of evidence.

That's my Dad! she thought, smiling fondly down at his reclining figure. There wouldn't be money enough in the world to buy him off, even if he were a poor man. He was of the old school to whom the words 'honor' and 'integrity' had real meaning. A truly incorruptible man. A man who would literally choose death before dishonor. And who, therefore, was always at risk. But didn't the fear of death upset him at all? He had simply shrugged off Petrosino's threats of vengeance, considering them part of the job—'an occupational hazard, dear.'

Tears unexpectedly stung her eyes as she surveyed the vulnerable figure before her. She loved him so much. Nothing must happen to

59

him, ever! She kissed his cheek lightly and murmured, 'I'll be outside,' not sure whether he had heard. As close as they were, none of them was a clinger. Each had a strong streak of independence and self-sufficiency. She knew he wouldn't mind her running off like this.

As she moved outside, the delightfully cool air lifted her auburn hair. She raised her face to the breeze and shook her head gently, reveling in the feel of it. What a refreshing change from the summer heat they had left behind.

All the deck chairs seemed to be occupied. Leonie hesitated outside the doorway evaluating the situation. What about that one, next to the two men deep in conversation? Had someone overlooked the jacket, or was it to reserve the chair? She moved to it and stood a moment, undecided. She really did want to sit outside for a while.

A gust blew her hair into her face, and as she raised a hand to clear it, the motion caught the eye of the man nearer her, an elderly, scholarly-looking type. He got up, apologetically grabbing the jacket. 'Oh, I'm so sorry. Would you like to sit here? I didn't mean to appropriate two chairs. I'm afraid I get carried away when I start talking.'

He had slouched to his feet, unfolding to an astonishing rail-thin height, an Ichabod Crane of a man. Now he gave Leonie a courtly little bow that was of another era. His thin face, homely but interesting and full of character, reminded her of an intelligent greyhound. Clear gray eyes sparkled behind old-fashioned steel-rimmed glasses. You quite forgot the rest of him when you looked into those eyes.

'Please do join me,' he begged Leonie, 'and I promise to stop expounding.' He shook his untidy head in a humorous gesture of mock despair. 'Although that won't be easy.' He smiled a crooked little smile, and Leonie smiled back immediately. She couldn't imagine anyone not smiling back at him, and decided she liked him very much.

'Oh, forgive me,' he went on. 'I'm forgetting my manners as well. I'm Dr. Morton Barnes, and this is . . .'

'We've met,' a deep voice interrupted.

Leonie knew who it was before she turned her head. That unmistakable voice! She nodded briefly toward the handsome Irishman who had rescued her from the locked cabin earlier that morning, then turned back to the other man. 'I'm Leonie Warwick,' she said. At the moment it simply did not occur to her that the younger man had never given his name. She had been busy stiffening her defenses when he trained those incredible blue eyes squarely on hers. But even as she noted the omission now, she dismissed it as he started to speak.

61

'Dr. Barnes is a geologist,' he was saying. 'He's been explaining how these hills got their unusual shapes. And we're in luck, because he's part of the teaching staff on the cruise. I never knew geology could be so interesting.'

'I'm afraid I interrupted your explanation, Dr. Barnes,' Leonie apologized.

'Not at all,' the geologist assured her. 'As I said, I'm afraid I get carried away and can't stop talking when I get on the subject. Probably bore everyone to death.' He ducked his head shyly, like a grotesquely overgrown little boy.

'Far from it,' the Irishman said. 'I wish you'd finish. I'll bet Miss Warwick would be interested too.'

'Oh, I really would,' Leonie agreed, with all sincerity. 'I've always gotten a lot more pleasure from my travels when I knew what I was looking at. And I'm not always lucky enough to have an expert on hand.'

Dr. Barnes beamed, dazzled more by Leonie's fabulous smile than by her genuine interest. 'Well, you see,' he began, with the eagerness of the born teacher, 'these sloping hills show the direction of the ice flow to the south during the Ice Age.' He gestured across the fjord-like channel. 'Working like sandpaper, the ice broke away cracks until the edges rounded off. It's called a *roche moutonnée*.'

'Sheep rock?' Leonie said, incredulous.

'Oh,' he said delightedly, 'you know French?'

'Not really,' Leonie admitted, 'but I've studied it some.'

'Well, I haven't,' the Irishman broke in, with his charmer's smile. 'Would somebody please explain what rocks have to do with sheep?'

'It's a delightful story,' Dr. Barnes said. 'In French, they're known as "fleecy rocks," in English, "sheepback," and they're supposed to remind you of sheep when you looked down on them, humped over at rest down in the valley. The term came from shepherds of the Pyrenees. It's one of the things I'll use in my lecture this afternoon. I hope you will both come.' His voice held the note of a youngster begging his busy mother to come see the new puppies. There was yearning, but not much hope. These extremely handsome young people spending time at a lecture? To his surprise, both his companions accepted without hesitation.

'I'd love to,' Leonie said. 'I truly enjoy things like that.'

'And I have a lot to learn on the subject,' the Irishman answered.

'Marvelous!' Dr. Barnes beamed on them like a doting parent. He could imagine a young man putting up with a great deal more than a geology lecture to spend some time next to *that* young lady! 'I'll see you both

63

later, then,' he said. 'I really must go and work on my notes some more.' Somehow he lifted all of his prodigious length against gravity again, smiled fondly down at them once more, and left.

Leonie could never remember exactly what she and the black-haired man talked about during the next hour or so, but she could feel her tension slipping away, and with it the restraint she had felt in his presence. She was no longer on guard, but relaxed and very much at ease. Maybe he was just 'playing it cool,' following some game plan of his own. She only knew that she was completely content to feel his closeness and lose herself in that magical voice.

CHAPTER SEVEN

CAPTIVATE...
to fascinate; to have special charm or beauty.

It seemed the most natural thing in the world for Irish to be waiting for her when Leonie met her parents in Purser's Square as they got ready to disembark the next morning in Prince Rupert.

Purser's Square was the designation given the open area in front of the dining room between the purser's office and the exit, and a throng of people milled about, securing the ID cards necessary to get on and off the ship.

Although they had moved breakfast ahead one hour because of their early arrival in Prince Rupert, Leonie felt fine. She thought with amazement of the many nights when she had slept a drugged sleep of nine or ten hours only to wake up feeling exhausted. She realized now that she had simply been unwilling to face another day and its problems. This morning she was fresh and eager after only a few hours' sleep.

The Irishman's piercing blue eyes drank in her loveliness as she moved toward him as unselfconsciously as if they had been friends for years. A strange feeling gripped him, and he realized with a feeling of astonishment that it was a pang of conscience. His type of work had not allowed for much of that. Business was business, and much of it pretty grim at times. But there was something about this Warwick girl that made deception more difficult than he had anticipated. Yet it was essential that she be unaware of his true identity. He had a part to play, a job to do. Nothing must interfere with that. Not even Leonie Warwick. His handsome face showed only a light-hearted gaiety as Leonie drew nearer.

'Well!' he said, eyeing her elegant outfit. 'I see your finery didn't turn to rags when we stopped dancing at the stroke of midnight.'

'And you don't look much like a pumpkin either!' Leonie retorted.

'Sorry, my girl,' he said in haughty tones, 'but you have your characters confused. I was the Prince Charming, not the waiting carriage.' They were both laughing merrily as John and Sanna approached in time to hear the last of the conversation.

'He certainly is a Prince Charming,' the judge muttered under his breath, 'but I hope Leonie's not moving too fast. She's so vulnerable now, and this chap could be another heartbreaker. Either one of them, for that matter. She danced all the first night with the big blond one, last night with this handsome devil. Maybe they're taking turns!'

'Oh, John,' Sanna murmured. 'See how happy she looks! Let her enjoy herself. She'll probably never see them again after the cruise ends. You know how these things go. I'm so delighted to see her having a good time again after ... after ...' She broke off, her voice cracking in spite of herself.

'Now, Sanna,' soothed the judge, 'you promised. You're not even to think about these past months. She does look happy. Let's keep it that way.' His voice changed, growing hearty as they drew abreast of the young couple. 'Well, good morning! You two look ready to conquer the world. Make that three,' he amended, smiling, as Werner Heinsohn suddenly joined the group, radiating enormous strength and animal vitality.

Leonie turned to her father indicating the dark-haired man. 'This is the man I attended Dr. Barnes' lecture with. You haven't met him yet.' She cocked a quizzical eyebrow. 'He has a proper name, but he says we're to call him "Irish," like everybody else.'

'That's good enough for me,' John Warwick said easily, as they shook hands, but something began to stir in the back of his mind.

'You met Werner Heinsohn the first night,' Leonie continued. 'In the Main Lounge, before the dancing.' She turned to the blond Viking.

'Before that, really,' the judge laughed. 'We had something of an introduction that first afternoon on the way to the Prom Deck.'

Leonie laughed. 'That's what you call bowling a girl over at first sight.'

But John Warwick's laughter was a little forced as he recalled the mystery surrounding Heinsohn's possession of the clipping, and the queer expression on the man's face as he recognized Leonie as the girl in the picture. Do we have *two* mystery men here? he wondered.

He turned his attention back to Irish, considering the younger man's old-fashioned courtesy, his air of distinction, his Ivy League accent. Could all that be an elaborate put-on, an act? but for what purpose? Perhaps he was being too critical, too protective of Leonie. He only knew he would do everything in his power to keep her from ever being hurt so badly again. At any rate, these chaps seemed suitable enough and, as Sanna had so reasonably pointed out, they were friendships that would merely last for the length of the cruise.

He shook his head mentally, determined to remember that this was his vacation too, and he needed to put aside his everyday habits of weighing evidence and judging people. 'How much time do we have in Prince Rupert?' he asked.

'We have to be back on board about noon, sir,' Irish answered, 'but I'm sure we'll have plenty of time for all we want to do. There's the museum, and a brief tour of the city, and that's about it, sir.'

John Warwick made a sudden decision. If these chaps were going to squire Leonie around, he'd like to get better acquainted. He said on impulse, 'Would you like to accompany us on this excursion?'

Heinsohn spoke first. 'Thank you very much, but I have another commitment. I just wanted to say hello. I'll see you all later.' But they saw nothing of him again until they were back for lunch after the tour.

Leonie was puzzled. A commitment? In a foreign port? That was strange. She felt a tiny stab of disappointment, then chided herself. Leonie Warwick, you are really too much! It's not enough you have the attention of the two most attractive men on board, but you think you have to appropriate all their time. Really! There was a tiny grin of self-mockery as she turned to hear Irish's answer to her father's invitation.

'Thank you, sir. I'd like that very much.' There was an air of quiet determination about this younge fellow that gave John Warwick the distinct impression that he would have found a way to accompany them without an invitation.

In the brief time before they moved toward the exit and disembarkation in Prince Rupert, Leonie thought: How strange that he can change so suddenly. One minute he's brash and bold, the sweep-you-off-your-feet type, then he's quiet and well-behaved. A sudden flash of insight illuminated her mind. Why, she told herself, the difference is whether or not Heinsohn is with us. Now there's a puzzler for you!

The judge, watching her careful assessment of the dark-haired man from under her thick lashes, gave an inaudible sigh and thought: be reasonable now, Dad. After all, Leonie is a very pretty girl. He shrugged off further evaluation as he followed his little group ashore.

Irish handed Leonie and Sanna down from

the gangplank with attentive care and threw out an expansive arm. 'Welcome to Prince Rupert, the halibut capital of the world.'

'Halibut? I thought Alaska was famous for its salmon,' Leonie said.

'So it is, but salmon is the glamour fish. Halibut is the money fish. But we're not in Alaska yet, you know. This is British Columbia, Canada. Tomorrow, when we reach Juneau, we'll be in Alaska, back in the United States.'

'Mother told me that. Why can't I remember it?'

'Speaking of fish,' Sanna said, joining the conversation, 'I'd love to send some home, but Myra Seton told me it's terribly expensive up here, and shipping prices are astronomical.'

'I think you'd best just enjoy it all while we're here,' her husband advised. 'Here are the buses. Sanna, how about being our guide? You're the one who went to all those lectures to get educated while the rest of us were lazing around.' He winked at Leonie and Irish.

'I presume that you mean in the museum,' his wife replied dryly. 'The bus driver will be our guide for the tour of the city. He's a pro.'

The judge laughed and tweaked her nose. 'Okay. When we get to the museum you can tell us what we want to spend our time on.'

'From what I heard at the lecture,' Sanna

said, after they were seated in the bus, 'the wolf mask and the bentwood boxes are what interest me the most. I don't know about the rest of you.'

'What in the world is a bentwood box?' Leonie wanted to know.

'It's just what it says,' her mother informed her. 'And they are fascinating.' Her face was alight with lively interest as she went on. 'They're made with strips of cedar that they steam and bend into forms. They secure the corners with thread or pegging so that there is just one seam. There is a great deal of art involved, as well as craft skills, and the lecturer said they sell for five, ten or even fifteen thousand dollars each. Imagine!'

Leonie's eyebrows flew upward. 'Take two, they're small.' She marveled at her own light-heartedness.

The weather matched her mood. The day was gloriously sunny, with temperatures in the seventies as they reluctantly left the view of the magnificent harbor. The guide was the first of many who were to tell them how rare such days were here. Their brief look at the city produced sights never seen at home: totem poles, moss on the roofs of the houses, and driveways so steep they actually had stair-like serrations in the concrete to make it possible to get the cars out in winter weather.

Inside the entrance to the Museum of Northern British Columbia, Leonie stared at

71

an odd-looking piece of machinery, trimmed in baby blue and complete with canopy, exhibited in a chained-off area. 'What a funny-looking little engine!'

John Warwick burst out laughing. 'Honey, that's not an engine. It's an old steam roller. A real honest-to-gosh steam roller. You don't see them around any more.'

'I guess that's why it's in a museum,' Leonie teased.

'And look at the beautiful flowers!' cried Sanna, the avid gardener. Her face was full of delight as she knelt by the colorful bed flanking the museum's inner entrance. 'They're just everywhere. What a lot of work they put in for such a short growing season. With the extra-long hours of light the colors are so brilliant. But we are so spoiled by our long summers in the Lower Forty-eight, as the natives call it.'

'Even their weeds are beautiful,' Leonie laughed. 'Remember those tall, colorful wildflowers we saw at the harbor?'

'You're forgetting that a weed is simply a plant that's out of place, or undesirable,' Irish reminded her. 'One man's weed is another man's bouquet. That's fireweed. It grows rampant in these parts. Legend has it that the height of the fireweed in summer determines the depth of the snow in winter.'

'How interesting.' Sanna looked at him with speculation. 'Have you been here before,

72

then?'

'No, I haven't,' Irish answered, then changed the subject neatly. 'Who knows who Prince Rupert was?' he asked before she could question him further. 'I read somewhere that a lady from Winnipeg won a prize of $250 for naming the town.'

'Address all queries to Sanna Warwick, the walking enclyclopedia,' Leonie laughed. 'I'll bet she knows.'

'As a matter of fact, I do, Miss,' Sanna retorted smartly, making a face at her teasing daughter. 'He was a cousin of Charles II of England, and was appointed by the British royal family to be the first governor of the Hudson's Bay Company. Which reminds me. When we stop in town, I want to go to the Pride of the North Mall they told us about, to see if I can afford one of those gorgeous Hudson's Bay point blankets.'

'And what, may I ask, is a Hudson Bay point blanket?' Leonie demanded. 'You mentioned those yesterday.'

'It's Hudson's Bay,' Sanna corrected gently. 'That is, if you're talking about the company. Although the body of water is Hudson Bay. The company and its blankets are world famous. Back in 1779, the Hudson's Bay Company introduced the point blanket for trade with the natives. The "points" are the short indigo lines marked on one edge, and they represented the number of beaver pelts demanded in exchange. Nowadays, the points mark the size. Otherwise, they're identical to the ones traded two hundred years ago—woven in England of the finest pure virgin wool. They're expensive, but they last a lifetime.'

By the time they returned to the ship at noon-time, Sanna had her blanket and they were discussing the sights that had impressed them most. All agreed that the museum exhibits and the totem poles of the Haida Indians took first place. After that, each had a preference. The judge declared his day had been made by the sight of the old steam roller and the impressive doorway of the Court of Justice, where he helpfully translated the Latin phrase above the door as: 'Hopefully, justice will be done.'

Irish had been intrigued by the horse's snowshoe displayed in the museum—a large iron ring with chain links leading to a smaller center ring. 'Imagine! A snowshoe for horses!' He shook his head wonderingly.

'That's not so strange,' Leonie said, 'when you consider the average rainfall here is ninety-one inches, and that's an average of two hundred and twenty days of precipitation! No wonder everyone's telling us how lucky we are to have the first clear day in weeks!' She laughed at her mother's sudden look of interest. 'Surprised you, didn't I, Mom? I'm not as gung-ho as you, but I did look up a few facts, too. What impressed you the most?'

'I'll tell only if you promise not to laugh.'

'Why would we laugh at you?' Leonie was puzzled.

Sanna burst out laughing herself. 'Well, I have to laugh at it,' she confessed. 'With all the exotic sights here, all I can think of are those plain-old-vanilla houses they showed us, with *no* yard and the eaves actually touching the neighbors' on some, that they said sold for hundreds of thousands of dollars!'

'They're paying for that gorgeous view of the bay,' Leonie laughed, 'and did you hear the guide say that many were owned by fishermen? With most of the wives working in the canneries while the men fish, it's not unusual for a fisherman to own a house that costs that much.'

'With salmon selling for what it does, I can understand that!' Sanna remarked. 'I don't even ask what it is at home. But what did you like best, Leonie, the bentwood boxes?'

'Oh, they were fabulous, with all the gorgeous work and just one seam, but I was particularly taken with the shaman's "soul catcher."'

'I guess I missed that,' the judge said. 'I don't even know what a shaman is.'

'You would have if you'd come with me to that lecture,' his wife announced, poking him playfully.

'Don't fight, you two,' Leonie grinned. 'Hush, and let me show off what little I know.' She clasped her hands together, pursed her lips, and adopted a professorial air. 'The shaman was the tribe's healer and the symbol of its beliefs, because they had no formal religion as such. They did not believe in the devil per se, but did believe in bad influences. One of the shaman's responsibilities was to act as an exorcist. The "soul catcher" was his beautiful box, about seven inches long, inlaid with abalone shell. I thought the story was fascinating.'

'It was quite a full morning, wasn't it?' Sanna said. 'I'm ready for lunch. Haven't the meals been great so far?'

'Too good,' Leonie said ruefully. 'I've gotten my appetite back with a vengeance. What's on the schedule for this afternoon besides the usual cards, bridge-and-bingo routine in the two lounges?'

'They have five lounges on the ship. Did you know that?' Sanna said. 'In one of them they'll have an hour of taped classical music. I'd love that, but I can enjoy that at home. I believe I'll just find a chair on the Prom Deck and absorb this fabulous scenery. I can't believe there's anything in Europe that's any prettier.'

'But you'd like a chance to compare, right?' Leonie laughed.

'That will be my next choice, yes, if I can get your father to repeat this miracle and get away from his work again.' She pouted at her husband, then turned to Leonie's escort. 'Have you been to Europe, Mr ...' She faltered. Facts she could remember; names were something else.

He smiled down at her. 'No need to be formal. I'd be pleased if you'd call me "Irish," too.'

Sanna laughed, agreed, then repeated her question. 'Have you been to Europe then, Irish?'

'No, not really,' he answered enigmatically, then broke off with obvious relief as Leonie interrupted him.

'Oh, look!' she said. 'Here comes Werner Heinsohn. We haven't seen him since we left the ship.' Actually, she had barely seen him since the first night when he had monopolized her on the dance floor. Irish had done the same the night before, and she wondered now if Heinsohn could have been that easily discouraged by the competition. He didn't strike her as that type at all. But his first words soon answered that question.

'You're going to have to share the wealth, Callahan,' he joked, after greeting everyone. 'I haven't had a minute with Leonie all day.'

'Not my fault,' Irish said airily. 'It's every man for himself where fair damsels are concerned. You were slow off the mark this morning. Did you enjoy Prince Rupert?'

Inexplicably, Heinsohn threw him a sharp look that seemed to contain a flash of anger, but his voice was bland as he answered the seemingly innocent question noncommittally. 'Very interesting.'

John Warwick, whose interest was piqued by the subtle undercurrent running between the two young men, said, 'I wasn't sure you'd made the shore excursion.' He wondered how they could possibly have missed someone his size all morning. His curiosity about this man aroused, he asked, 'Will you be taking the tour in Juneau tomorrow?'

'Oh, yes,' the blond giant replied. 'I don't have a thing to do now but enjoy myself for the rest of the week. I mean, for two weeks,' he corrected himself hastily.

How strange, John Warwick thought. That was a funny thing to say. And that was a mighty funny look young Irish gave him when he said it. He was going to ask Sanna later if she had noticed the odd interplay between the two young men, then decided against it.

Come now, he scolded himself. There you go again, always looking for something suspect. Will you relax! Unconsciously, he shrugged his shoulders, as though trying to rid himself of a burden and said, 'Well, I am here to announce that I'm going to be much smarter tomorrow than I was today. I'm going to the lecture that tells us about Juneau this evening, and then I'll know as much as my wife does. She's been upstaging me all day. Can't let that happen, can we, boys!'

They all laughed, and Sanna said delightedly, 'Oh, good! The lecture's in the theater, and we can stay on to see the movie. It's one of Katharine Hepburn's old ones, and she's always been a favorite of mine.' She turned back to Irish. 'And will you be taking the tour in Juneau tomorrow, Mr ... er ... ?' She broke off with an embarrassed laugh. 'I'm sorry, but it seems strange to call you nothing but "Irish."'

For some reason he shot a quick look at John Warwick, then answered easily, 'But that's what I'm used to. As you've noticed, no one is very formal here.'

Now that was slick, John Warwick thought, and decided that he would, after all, pay more attention to the man he thought he had recognized when they had first boarded the ship. At the time, he had pushed the thought from his mind, chiding himself for being so slow to slough off the unpleasant memories associated with the Petrosino trial.

The young man had been careful not to give any name but 'Irish,' but hadn't young Heinsohn called him 'Callahan?' He searched his memory but could not be sure. Could this possibly be Tom Callahan? It certainly looked like him. But he'd been on the brink of death

79

shortly before they left. This man was absolutely vibrating with animal good health. He mentally shook his head, returning with an effort to the conversation at hand. Couldn't be, he told himself firmly. Or could it? Modern drugs sometimes worked near-miracles.

They soon separated to get ready for lunch. Later, the lazy afternoon hours at sea drove all troublesome thoughts from even the judge's mind.

CHAPTER EIGHT

WAIT...
to stay or rest in expectation.

'Gold!' John Warwick's voice rang out dramatically as they sat at the breakfast table. 'Can you imagine the reaction to *that* announcement? How I would love to have been there at Silver Bow Basin on Gold Creek in the summer of 1880 to see the looks on the faces of old Joe Juneau and Dick Harris when they found it. Things were never the same again. From then until April 1944, when the big industrial operations ended, there were eleven mines in the Juneau and Douglas area working twenty-four hours a day. Can you imagine living in a day when five, ten and twenty-dollar gold pieces were common currency? I was reading an account by one of the old-timers, and he said you didn't see much silver or paper money those days. In the saloons and dance halls, most of the money that changed hands was gold. Can you conceive of the value, by today's gold prices, of all that stuff they threw round so freely!'

'Well, you'll get a chance to do just that, too,' Leonie said. 'At least in playacting. That is, if you'll join us in our rehearsal tonight for the Talent Show. Werner and Irish have already talked me into signing up. You'd make a perfect "Dan McGrew."'

'Aha!' the judge said, his eyes lighting up. 'Robert W. Service. One of my favorite poets. I have a hard time deciding which I like best, "The Shooting of Dan McGrew" or "The Cremation of Sam McGee." They both are corkers. When was all this decided?'

'Last night,' Leonie said, 'while you and mother were at the lecture on Juneau.'

Her mind went back to that meeting now, and what she remembered troubled her. She had appeared without warning on the Prom Deck and caught Irish and Werner Heinsohn with their deck chairs pulled close together, the dark head almost touching the blond one.

'Hi!' she had said breezily, then wondered why the startled men looked so guilty. They had been so intent on their conversation that they were not even aware of her approach.

81

'Why so surprised to see me?' she had asked.

'It's just . . . just that we thought you were with your folks,' Heinsohn stammered.

How odd to see the Iron Man flustered! 'You look like a couple of conspirators, plotting some dark deed,' she had said, laughing.

'We are,' Irish had replied promptly, his face so quickly animated by his dazzling smile and mischief-filled eyes that Leonie thought she must have imagined the fleeting grim expression that crossed it as she spoke.

Werner Heinsohn's face was perfectly bland, as expressionless as a bowl of vanilla pudding, until he, too, smiled. 'We were discussing a deep, dark secret,' he told her, 'but we're considering letting you in on it.'

'I'm honored,' Leonie had said dryly. 'But are you sure I can handle it? You know the old saw: "telegraph, telephone, tell a woman."'

They had both smiled in earnest then. 'Oh, yes!' Irish was emphatic. 'We know you can handle it. You are about to become . . .' He stopped while he flapped his heavy eyebrows wildly and leered in an exaggerated manner—'to become "the lady that's known as Lou!"'

'What!' Leonie had laughed and looked indulgent. They were like two small boys vying for her attention. 'Would someone mind telling me just what you two are talking about?'

Irish said, 'I guess you don't know the world's great poetry.' He struck a pose and began to recite. '"*A bunch of the boys were whooping it up at the Malamute Saloon ...*"'

'Oh, that! Of course I do. I just didn't remember the name.'

'That, my girl,' said Irish, 'is the classic by Robert W. Service: "The Shooting of Dangerous Dan McGrew"—a fellow Irishman, of course—and you will be dazzling as Lou, his light-of-love.'

Looking back now, as they sat in the dining room, Leonie's thoughts returned not to the laughter and joking, but to the grim intensity with which the men were talking as she took them unawares. Only in retrospect did it occur to her that the frivolity had seemed a bit strained and heavy-handed, a red herring to lure her away from the original mood. What in the world could they have been talking about?

'Why so serious, Leonie?' Her father's question interrupted her somber thoughts. 'Are you ...' He broke off as their waiter approached to take orders. Realizing that their proper names would be too difficult for English-speaking passengers, the Oriental waiters and stewards had taken American names. This young man was 'Robert.' It seemed very odd to address him that way, then hear him chatter in Mandarin Chinese to the other boys.

The judge had tried to learn some of the language. He said now, 'Ah, good morning, Robert. Or should I say *t'sow ahn*. There! How did I do?'

'Very well, sir, very well!' Robert was all teeth and sparkling eyes behind his large-rimmed glasses. No inscrutable Oriental here!

Leonie had her own opinion. 'Well, Dad, you didn't sound any worse than Charlie Beardsley, our Texan, when he's trying to talk Spanish to the Carrascos, that nice couple from Mexico City. You can almost see them cringe.'

'Well, thanks a lot!' her father said in mock indignation. 'I thought I was doing pretty well. You're not even trying it. Now you just listen and you can be properly impressed.' He turned back to Robert. '*Ni how*? How are you?'

Robert beamed and bobbed. '*How di. Shin shin ni*. Fine, thank you.'

'*Buo chih*,' said the judge. 'You're welcome.' And he gave grave little bows around the table, acknowledging the wild applause from his family that followed. Many heads, turning at the sounds of gaiety, looked with envy at the distinguished-looking couple and their beautiful daughter.

But after the meal was served, John

Warwick again watched his daughter thoughtfully. 'You're not eating, Leonie. Are you all right?'

'Oh, Daddy, I'm stuffed from last night.' She kept her tone light, but was careful not to look directly at him. There wasn't much got by that gentleman!

'Let me refresh your memory,' she continued, trying to distract his attention. 'We had shrimp cocktail, cream of onion soup, red snapper, baked potato, broccoli, salad and apple pie. And you expect me to be hungry again this morning?'

The judge, not easily diverted from the evidence at hand, was quite aware she was not meeting his eyes. 'Is there something bothering you, Leonie?'

She did look at him then, her decisions made. 'Not really. I thought there was a problem, but I guess I was mistaken.'

Her father, never one to pry or ask personal questions, let the matter drop there and steered the conversation into safer channels.

'We have to tender in Juneau,' he informed them. 'That should be fun.'

'I'm not sure what you mean, John,' Sanna said hesitantly. It bothered her to have him use a word she didn't know.

He explained. 'Some of the places we visit will either lack docking facilities or water deep enough to accommodate the cruise ship,

85

so they will use small boats—tenders—to transfer passengers from the ship to the shore, and someone decided to make a verb out of it, as they do with so many words nowadays.' The conversation was very general after that until they finished their meal and went up to the Prom Deck to get their first look at Alaska.

There were mixed reactions as the ship gracefully glided within sight of Juneau.

'Alyeska,' Sanna sighed, her eyes shining with emotion. 'The Great Land!'

'Sold to us for about two cents an acre!' the judge added dryly.

Charlie Beardsley, the genial feed store owner from Texas, bounced his roly-poly figure up and down on the tips of his cowboy boots like a child in anticipation of a great treat. 'Look at this place!' His eyes gleamed at the sight of the city crowded in between the water and the towering mountains, which to outsiders appear encroaching. 'Talk about the pioneer spirit! There they are, backed up into a wall of mountain, like a boxer with his dukes up, taking on the world. And talk about originality! If you want to bring a car, it has to come aboard one of the State-operated ferries. You can't even drive into the place.'

Leonie eyed the city teetering on a narrow ledge of land, sandwiched in between boundless waters and massive ranges and said, 'I wonder how much moisture it takes to make all this gorgeous greenery.'

Dr. Barnes, standing beside her, laughed as he said, 'Would it answer your question if I told you this is our first day of sunshine in six weeks?' He turned to Beardsley. 'I just hope you folks from the Sun Belt have brought some with you that will stay. We outdid ourselves this year where rain is concerned.'

'That doesn't seem to discourage the tourists,' Sanna commented.

'You're right,' Barnes said. 'When the Aleuts told the Russians the mainland was Alyeska, the Great Land of White to the east, they really meant it. Not only is it more than twice the size of Texas,' he broke off to grin at Beardsley, 'but west of Juneau and north of Glacier Bay there is one glacier alone that is bigger than the whole state of Rhode Island. Not to mention seventy-five pound cabbages and beets the size of your head. The long daylight hours result in some fantastic produce.'

John Warwick turned a mock-lugubrious look on the jolly man from Amarillo. 'Sorry, Charlie. I don't know what this is going to do to your Texan boasts.'

'Never mind,' Beardsley laughed good-naturedly. 'We've still got armadillos and the Dallas Cowboys! But look over yonder. We're missing the sights.'

'That's the old Alaska-Juneau mine!' the judge said excitedly.

87

'There she is,' Dr. Barnes said. 'In her day, the old A-J put out over ten thousand tons of ore *every day*, and by the time she closed in 1944 she had produced eighty-one million worth of gold. She and the Treadwell Mine on Douglas Island were two of the greatest gold mines the world has ever seen. And there's still "gold in them thar hills,"' he added with an exaggerated hillbilly drawl. 'When we land, you'll see a big sign on Merchant's Wharf. "Pan for Gold." You might want to try your hand at it yourselves. Many people don't realize that Alaska is experiencing a new gold rush since the price of precious metals has skyrocketed. Have you ever seen the huge dredges they used in the interior to mine gold?'

'No,' the judge answered. 'Will we see some on the trip?'

'That depends. How far north are you going?'

'We're not taking the icecap flight, so we'll only go as far north as Anchorage. How about you folks, Charlie?'

'We're not taking it either. Guess we'll miss 'em, eh, Doc?'

'Well, you have to go north out of Fairbanks to get into the gold fields, so I guess you will miss them. But they are something to see. Monsters. Some of them higher than a forty-story building.'

'Are they still in use?' Beardsley asked.

'Costs rose so steadily after World War II they were completely gone by the early 1960's. However, I understand they have been reactivated in the Nome area. They're still producing gold there on a consistent basis. The Alaska Gold Company recovers several million in gold every year. But you won't get that far north either, will you?'

'I'm afraid not,' John Warwick said regretfully. 'Will that diminish our chances of seeing animals? One of the passengers was complaining the only wildlife she saw was the MGM lion in the movie theater! I'm afraid she expected them to be standing on every shore, lined up in formation for inspection.'

Barnes laughed along with the others, then said seriously, 'I hope she expected to see them only at a distance. I wonder what she'd do if she came across pawprints fourteen inches across, bigger than pie plates! People are killed and injured every year because they don't take seriously the warnings about wild animals. After all, they live here. *We* are the trespassers. And their attacks can be as sudden and violent as a williwaw.'

Sanna's ears perked up with interest. 'I've heard that word,' she said, 'but I'm not sure just what it is. All I know is that it's a big wind.'

'Must be the Alaskan equivalent of a Texas blue norther,' Charlie Beardsley chuckled.

'Not really,' Dr. Barnes corrected, 'because

there is no frontal system. These winds are caused by perpendicular drafts near a glacier or open tundra, blowing down over the cold terrain, then over a large body of water.

'I remember once, when I was younger, a friend and I took our kayak out. Here we were on a beautifully calm, clear lake, framed by magnificent forests against a backdrop of snow-crowned mountains. Idyllic. The only significant cloud seemed far away. It moved so slowly we took little notice until the wind slapped us and the heavens opened up. Try paddling a kayak in a fifty-mile-an-hour wind! And that was just an ordinary williwaw. They can reach as high as one hundred miles an hour.'

Morton Barnes stopped and smiled his engaging smile. 'Well, forgive me, I'm lecturing again. And, what's worse, I'm beginning to sound like a typical Alaskan talking down to a Cheechako—a newcomer. I'm afraid we take ourselves much too seriously. I'll hush now and let you enjoy Juneau.' He waved to the group and was gone.

CHAPTER NINE

PROLONG...
to lengthen in duration.

'We're retarded today,' Irish announced as he joined the Warwicks. As usual he had eyes only for Leonie. He strode directly to her side, his bold glance detailing every highlight of her stunning figure. She did her best to act cool and a little aloof in the face of his brashness, but could feel herself respond to his overwhelming masculinity and the exuberance of his animal-healthy vitality.

The whole atmosphere seemed charged when he appeared on the scene. She could actually feel the change. It was the same sensation of immense stored power she experienced when tension built up before a thunderstorm. She thought wryly, I'll have to be careful not to get struck by lightning! Helpless to resist his enormous appeal, she was determined not to show her reaction.

She cocked an inquiring eyebrow at him and felt the full impact of his magnetism as he turned those incredible eyes of startling Irish blue full on her. 'Don't look at me like that,' he laughed. 'Didn't you see the sign? It told us to retard our watches one hour. We're on Yukon Time here. I believe we make four changes all told during the trip.'

'Worse than Daylight Saving,' Leonie grumbled.

'Well, don't growl at me. You can blame old Ben Franklin for that one. He invented it, you know. But he didn't have much to do with this old world's geography, so don't blame him for that.'

'That's right, Leonie,' the judge added. 'Be fair.'

Leonie laughed and took a poke at him. It was so good to see him so completely relaxed, so unlike his usual formal and dignified self. Strangely enough, this was mostly evident when Irish was around. He seemed to react to the ebullient Irishman's light-hearted banter by relaxing visibly. Yet she had caught him stealing speculative glances at the younger man on several occasions, as if trying to determine something. They were looks of assessment, as if he were trying to make a judgment on the man who was so obviously taken with his daughter. Surely he wasn't surveying him with the eye of a prospective father-in-law! He himself had warned her it was not wise to get involved too seriously with shipboard acquaintances. She had given up the fight within herself much earlier and decided there was no reason why she should not enjoy Irish's company for the sheer pleasure of being near him. His wit and humor had already done much to dispel the dark shadows lingering from the past as she began the cruise. Her whole attitude had changed strikingly in the few days she had known him. But for now she'd let him know that he was not the only attractive man available.

'Where's Werner Heinsohn?' she asked him.

'He went to ask if we could use the stage to practice our skit for the Talent Show. The band doesn't start playing until eight, and because of our tours in Juneau there will be an open buffet instead of the usual seating. So we could eat early, right after we come back on board, and then get together to rehearse. What do you say?'

'That's fine with me,' Leonie said. 'How about you, Dad? You're practically the star of the show. Oh, that reminds me. We forgot to ask you, Mom, if you'd be willing to play the piano for us. Would you? The only costume you'd need would be something to make you look like a boy. That won't be hard to find. The poem mentions "the kid that handles the music-box." You could stuff your hair under a cap and wear a false mustache.'

'One prop we'll have to find for ourselves, because the costume box doesn't have it, is a false beard,' Irish said. 'Since the judge takes the part of "the stranger," he'll have to be sure he's not recognizable. The poem describes him as having "a face most hair", so we'll have to find a beard that covers most of his face. The whole idea is that at first nobody can figure out who he is when he staggers into the saloon.'

'What will we do for guns?' the judge wanted to know. 'If you and I are to kill each other in the play, we'll each have to have some kind of firearm. And, furthermore, it will have to be one that makes a proper noise, because when the narrator gets to the action part it says something about the lights going out and two guns blazing in the dark.'

'That's why we'll need several rehearsals, sir,' Irish said. 'The timing there has to be just right. So we'll have to find someone to help with the lights backstage and coordinate all that. The timing will be crucial.'

'We'll all look around for a beard in Juneau,' the judge said. 'Will you be coming with us to see what they call the Southeast's "drive-in glacier?"'

'Oh, I wouldn't miss the Mendenhall Glacier,' Irish answered. 'It's only a few miles from town, they say. Imagine having a glacier in your back yard! And how about the Mendenhall Glacier Float Trip! Are any of you taking that?'

'Well, I for one am,' John Warwick said emphatically, 'in spite of my two worrywart women.' He smiled to soften the impact of his words, knowing Sanna's fussing was due to her concern for his health.

It was true he'd been under enormous strain throughout the long-drawn-out months of the Petrosino trial, but the doctor didn't seem concerned about his heart palpitations. 'Flutters,' he had called them, and didn't seem to think the little flare-up had been important. 'The isolation and relaxation of the cruise will be just the thing to relieve that tension,' he had promised. And it was true. Just being completely withdrawn from the preoccupations and pressures of his job had worked a minor miracle. He was, as he kept telling his family, 'rarin' to go!' Now he smiled again at Leonie's worried little frown and Sanna's open anxiety.

'Oh, John, are you really going to take that raft trip down the rapids when we get to Juneau?' Sanna pleaded.

'Why, I'm looking forward to it!' he assured her. 'Surely you're not worried about that? You know what Dr. Emerson said. Why don't you change your mind and come with us, dear?'

'No, thanks,' Sanna said hastily. 'I'll go with you to see the Mendenhall Glacier, of course, but no Float Trips for me. I'm not sure I want you two to go.'

'Oh, Mother!' Leonie protested. 'They do this all the time. I don't think they've lost anyone yet!'

'I suppose not,' Sanna agreed reluctantly, 'but I'm sure it could be dangerous.'

'Anything can, so far as that goes,' Leonie reminded her. 'You know you take your life in your hands every time you step into the car when you're at home. But I was talking to one of the staff about this, and he tells me the young men who handle the rafts are very carefully trained. To be honest, I was a little hesitant about it myself. But he assured me they spend many weeks running the rapids, first with someone experienced, then by themselves, and finally with the other men as test passengers. They make certain they know what they're doing before they give them the responsibility of a raft full of tourists.'

'Oh, I don't doubt that a bit,' Sanna said, 'but I'm afraid your father will get carried away with all of this. There is so much to see and do, and the days are so long. He tends to forget his job is mostly sedentary and chockfull of pressures. Then, too, there is always the unexpected on that kind of adventure.' Her words were to prove prophetic.

The judge, of course, was listening to all this, but was not the least impressed. 'Poor woman,' he sniffed. 'She's been intimidated by the lecturer who said that in Alaska just staying up until dark takes endurance!'

The resulting laughter lightened the mood and Sanna gave in gracefully. 'I give up,' she said. 'To quote James Russell Lowell, "There is no good in arguing with the inevitable. The

96

only argument available with an east wind is to put on your overcoat."' She turned to Leonie and said with pretended accusation, 'Here you are aiding and abetting him, and I thought the idea of shooting the rapids terrified you.'

'Who expects a woman to be reasonable?' the judge asked of no one in particular, but gave Irish a sly wink as he spoke. 'I can quote, too,' he went on. 'A man by the improbable name of Coventry Patmore once said, "A woman is a foreign land, / Of which, though there he settle young, / A man will ne'er quite understand / The customs, politics and tongue."'

'How much time will we have in Juneau?' Leonie asked, awarding her father's remark only a supercilious look with suddenly lowered lashes and exaggeratedly pulled-down mouth. 'Can we do some sightseeing too, or will there just be time for the glacier and raft trip?'

'Well, let's see,' her father said. 'Since we have first seating, we can eat as early as 11:30, and we don't have to meet on the dock for the Mendenhall Glacier trip until a little after 2:00. If we can get on that first tender, we should have some extra time. But we'll have to have our ID cards ready and be right up front at the door. The seating capacity is only sixty passengers.'

'What ID cards are you talking about,

Dad? I must have missed something in the notices,' Leonie said.

'There'll be a manifest posted in Purser's Square,' the judge said, 'to tell you what number you've been issued. We have to take these cards with us every time we leave the ship, then return them to the rack when we come back. It's the only way they have of knowing who is on the ship for sailing, for messages, or in case of emergency.'

'Will we have time to see the House of Wickersham?' Sanna asked. 'I was reading up on it and they said it is a fine old home on Seventh Street which houses the largest and finest collection of Alaskana-historical books, diaries, documents, early artifacts and treasures dating back to the Russian-American days. Wouldn't that be interesting?'

'Indeed it would,' her husband agreed. 'Would that be the home of Judge James Wickersham? He was one of Alaska's outstanding statesmen and historians. And he was also a pioneer judge and delegate to Congress. I was reading something about him myself the other day. It was most interesting. Let's see, what was it that I found up in the library? Oh, yes, I remember. In the winter of 1904, Judge Wickersham traveled by dog team over an unblazed trail all the way from Valdez to Fairbanks in fourteen days. That was a distance of three hundred and seventy

98

miles. Then, in 1932, he went over the same trail by automobile, plus the one hundred and sixty miles from Fairbanks to Circle, a total distance of five hundred and thirty miles, in fewer than three days. And, of course, in 1932 they didn't have the faster cars and the highways we have now.'

'That's what civilization can do for you, Dad,' Leonie teased him.

He was not about to let her get ahead of him. 'And I expect that "woman will be the last thing civilized by man,"' he informed her, then ducked in mock apprehension. 'Don't hit me! That wasn't even original. George Meredith said it in *Richard Feverel*. Blame him.'

As they disbanded for lunch, Leonie's heart soared at her father's light-heartedness, her own feeling of well-being, and the prospect of an exciting afternoon with Irish.

CHAPTER TEN

DISSIMULATE...
to disguise or conceal one's true intentions.

Leonie's spirits rose with every mile they covered. The gentle motion of the ship, the rich blending of the blues of water and sky, the misty islands and the graceful gulls wheeling overhead were all a soothing balm to her troubled soul. She could feel turmoil and turbulence fading, and the days ahead seemed filled with hope and promise. She sat by the hour, watching as row upon row of mounded hills and mountains thick with pines, passed in review, rising directly out of the water on either side.

By the time they had caught the early tender over to Juneau and completed their tour of the city, she was bubbling with excitement as the tour bus began the short trip out of town to the Mendenhall Glacier. On the way the Warwicks compared notes.

'What did you like best, Dad?' Leonie asked.

'Well,' the judge said, 'it's the first time I've been in a city where the stairs made sidewalks. Many of them are actually streets, with street names.'

'That was quaint,' she agreed. 'I think I was most impressed with the spectacular view from the terraces off the lobby of the eighth floor in that dramatic State Office Building. That was certainly not one of your old-timers! All that glass and concrete! And wasn't that organ something! They said it was a restored 1928 Kimball Theater organ. How about you, Mom? What impressed you?'

Sanna laughed. 'I thought the whole Governor's Mansion with its pillars was beautiful, but what really impressed me was that it was built back in 1912 for only $40,000 *including* furnishings! Can you imagine? And I liked the St. Nicholas Russian Orthodox Church. Such an odd shape. Very picturesque and distinctly old Russian.'

'Where was it we saw that unpainted totem pole?' Leonie wanted to know.

'That was the Juneau Memorial Library,' Sanna replied. 'The lecturer said last night that was a Tlingit Totem Pole, carved by Amos Wallace for the 1967 Alaska Centennial.'

'Oh! I've been mispronouncing that name. So it's "klink-it?" I was wondering about that.'

Sanna pretended severity as she leaned closer to Leonie in the next seat and hissed in a low tone, 'You'd be better informed, young lady, if you went to lectures instead of cavorting with good-looking men of an evening.' They giggled like a couple of schoolgirls, bringing raised eyebrows and curious glances from John across the aisle from them, and Irish, who turned from his seat in front of Leonie.

What a close family they are, he thought, and wished he were a thousand miles away instead of being here under false pretenses with a difficult assignment.

'Why are we stopping?' the judge asked.

His question was answered in a moment when the bus driver, who was also their tour

101

guide, said, 'We'll stop for just a few minutes here at the Mendenhall River so that you can see the salmon spawning.'

They trooped out briskly, eager to see such an exotic sight. The guide explained that the salmon spawned from August through October, then died, leaving abundant and easily accessible food for the bears. Scores of pictures were taken in the brief time they watched the beautiful fish moving lazily in the clear, shallow water. Then, as they moved back to the bus, John burst out laughing. When three pairs of curious eyes asked, 'What's the joke?' he explained. 'I was just thinking about something Morton Barnes told me earlier. He told some yarn about the city fathers here deciding they would clean up the town and ordering all the prostitutes out. When they moved, all the fishermen followed them, up to Ketchikan. He concluded by saying that when Creek Street in Ketchikan was a red-light district, it was known for years as "the only spot in the world where men and fish go up the same creek to spawn!"

Sanna said, 'Oh, John!' in a tone of mild reproof, but she laughed along with the rest of them. He hugged her to him as they walked. 'Okay, Miss Priss. But I'm glad you're not so genteel you can't enjoy a bit of innocent humor. I'd hate to have a sourpuss for a wife!'

'How about a nag?' Sanna smiled up at him

102

mischievously, and he knew what was coming.

'Oh, no,' he groaned. 'Not the raft trip again!'

'I wish you'd remember,' she reminded him, 'that when you shoot those rapids on the Mendenhall River you'll be soaked with the melted water of a twelve-mile-long slab of ice that came down from a fifteen-hundred-square-mile icecap!'

'And I wish,' her husband said dryly, 'you wouldn't be quite so big on statistics, dear. I'm having a great time, and I'm going to be just fine. Please don't fuss.'

Leonie interrupted her mother hastily, hoping to change a subject that was one of the rare bones of contention between her parents. She too had always worried about the effects of her father's grueling schedule on his health, and knew he was entirely too nonchalant about it. But she did not want Sanna worrying about a thing on this trip, expecially when the burden of her daughter's unhappiness was finally beginning to lift.

She slipped an arm through her mother's, keeping her tone light. 'It's okay, Mom,' she said. 'If he overdoes things we'll just send him back to that place especially for senior citizens that we saw in Vancouver.'

'I didn't see...' Sanna began, her tone darkly mistrustful, then stopped as she realized her suspicions, as usual, were justified. 'All right, you two, I'll bite. Far be it from me to spoil your fun.'

Leonie managed to look the wide-eyed innocent as she continued. 'You know, the one back on the strip in Vancouver that was called "The Slipped Disco."'

'Wish I hadn't asked,' Sanna groaned, thinking how good it is to hear all of us laugh so freely again. And her family knew she would not bring up the subject of the raft trip again.

Back on the bus Leonie said, 'Can you imagine practically walking up to a glacier that's only thirteen miles from downtown? I find it very exciting. Do you suppose the natives get blasé about it? Dr. Barnes explained to us that snowfall on the icefield exceeds one hundred feet some years, and the tremendous pressure of the snow turns it into glacial ice.'

'If you can stand another one of my stories,' her father said, 'I learned something else about glaciers that I found interesting. Did you know that glacial ice is harder than other ice? Well, it is,' he answered the shaking heads, 'and it will stay in a glass longer. Just before Alaska and Hawaii became the forty-ninth and fiftieth states, the story is told of an Alaskan publisher flying an iceberg to Washington to make what he called the '49–50' cocktail. Another publisher, delegate Farrington of Hawaii, had his picture taken drinking Hawaiian pineapple juice chilled with glacial ice.'

'Here we are, folks,' the bus driver called as he pulled the vehicle to a stop. 'We're at the end of Glacier Spur Road, which is at the end of Glacier Highway, which is all of forty miles long. We'll have a brief stop here so those of you who signed up for it can make the Float Trip on time. Have fun, and get good pictures.'

The group stood spellbound by their first glacier, awed by a head-on view of the magnificent river of ice, separated from them only by a narrow strip of water. Finally, Leonie broke the silence. 'How would you like to look out your kitchen window at *that* every day?'

'That would be something,' her father agreed. 'But living in Juneau might have its drawbacks too. In an area that has several months of nearly complete darkness you wouldn't see much of glaciers or anything else for long stretches. And I expect it would be about then you'd remember that all the roads in town simply don't go anywhere.'

They surveyed the beauty before them in silence. Then Leonie said, in the hushed tones usually reserved for magnificent cathedrals, 'Look at that incredible blue!'

'It is unusually vivid, isn't it?' Sanna agreed. 'Dr. Barnes explained in his lecture that the striking blue tone of glacial ice comes from six-sided ice crystals, highly compacted by the weight of accumulated snow, which refract only blue light.'

It was not long afterward that they stood selecting rain gear from a huge pile of equipment. Leonie, Irish, and the judge suited up in ponchos and boots, Leonie's much too big for her. Presumably it was better economics to have gear too big for the women than too small for the men.

It was very windy because of the turbulence created on a sunny day by the unusually warm air meeting the cold water. John looked askance at the twelve-foot raft bobbing up and down on the choppy water. By the time they finished loading there were ten people and the oarsman crowded into the small space.

The young man at the oars fought a terrific wind around three points of land before finally turning to enter the white water. Well trained in handling the turbulence of the water, he was clearly unused to the unexpected agitation of the air as well. The raft stayed in one spot for several anxious moments as he struggled with all his considerable strength without moving them forward one bit. Leonie began to feel nervous, and the judge began to wonder if he would have been smarter to listen to his wife after all.

Irish, pressed close to Leonie in the

cramped quarters, whispered, 'Do you think I should offer to help, or would he resent it? I don't think we want to go swimming in this.' Even he looked uneasy, unsure of another man's abilities where he seemed so very sure of his own.

Before she could reply, the oarsman seemed to get his second wind and the raft began to move again against the fierce gale. Then, just as they were maneuvering around a large rock, disaster struck. A wicked gust caught the raft unexpectedly, and one of the oars sprang right out of the oarlock. There were a frantic few seconds while Irish grabbed the oar and the oarsman, who had lost his balance and fallen back into Leonie's lap, struggling mightily to get fully back into his seat and regain control. The entire boatload had dire visions of their being the first casualties of the famed Mendenhall Float Trip. But the capable young man managed to get the maverick oar back in place and pushed away before they could crash into the rock.

Except for those anxious moments the rest of the trip was delightful. There was the roller-coaster excitement of lifting up and down on the waves, and the expected squeals, shouts and shrieks as the icy water washed over them and into the raft. In spite of the ponchos they were soon drenched, their boots full of cold water. Leonie was grateful for the unexpectedly warm day, even though it was the cause of their trouble in creating the conflict between air and water.

In the excitement of their brush with calamity, Leonie became more conscious than ever of Irish's closeness. Immediately after the frightening incident with the wayward oarlock he had put his arm protectively around her, and it seemed the most natural thing in the world to lean against his rock-hard chest and feel completely safe and protected. There were no shivers of fear, no negative reactions in her first close contact with a male body since she had escaped Walter. Bumping into Werner Heinsohn that first day didn't count. From the look of sheer astonishment on his face it was obvious that that encounter had been completely unplanned on his part.

Irish was acutely aware of Leonie's unconscious sigh of contentment and her instinctive snuggling against him, and felt the worst kind of hypocrite.

So completely at home did she feel in the circle of his arms, even with the wild bobbing of the raft on the rough water, that she felt a certain disappointment when they pulled in for a brief stop on a small beach.

Water was poured out of boots, and soaking socks were wrung out amid excited retellings of the gasps of consternation each time a wave washed over the occupants of the raft. Large round crackers were handed out bearing pieces of smoked salmon, reindeer sausage and cheese.

'But this is delicious!' Leonie exclaimed after the snacks had been identified. 'And what do you call these crackers? They're so different from anything I've ever had.'

'That's pilot bread,' their raft skipper told them. 'You can buy it locally. It's sold in long blue boxes with the label "Sailor Boy."'

'And the best is yet to come,' Irish informed her, handing her a paper cup. 'Have a little "Mendenhall Madness." They are dispensing a very special brew to keep us from getting mildewed.'

'What is this?' John asked. 'It's not cider and it's not wine. I just can't identify it, but it is a superlative drink.'

'I asked,' Irish told them. 'When I tasted it I just had to know how they concocted such ambrosia. It's a mixture of champagne and peach brandy!'

The remainder of the Float Trip was exhilarating but uneventful and Sanna, relieved to have them all back safe and sound, happily watched their animated faces as they relived the excitement of the adventure for her, carefully deleting the only time they had been in danger. She thought: how much younger John looks. I've never seen him look better. And as she watched Leonie she breathed a little prayer of thanks. The glow

109

was back! That lovely inner radiance which added an extra dimension to Leonie's physical beauty had been extinguished for so long. From the way her daughter looked at Irish it was plain to see that more than a cruise was responsible for the restoration.

There was such a look of gratitude on Sanna's face as she gave Irish the full benefit of her charming smile that he almost groaned aloud.

He returned it as best he could, hating himself, thinking: if they only knew!

CHAPTER ELEVEN

INCUBATE...
to cause to develop.

The next morning dawned bright and clear. 'How lucky we are to have this good weather continue,' Leonie said to her father. 'I've heard horror stories of people who took this trip only to find Glacier Bay socked in with fog or have it pouring down rain. I'm so grateful we'll be able to see everything.' She turned to Heinsohn, who had joined them after breakfast on the forward deck. It was the first she had seen of him since their discussion on the Prom Deck about 'The Shooting of Dan McGrew' for the Talent

Show.

'We lost you yesterday,' she said to the blond giant as he lowered his bulk carefully into the deck chair next to hers. 'You really missed something on that raft trip.'

'Exciting, eh?' He smiled his tight secretive little smile; his mind seemed to be elsewhere.

'Oh, it was marvelous!' she assured him. 'You should have been with us.'

'I had planned to,' he lied, 'but I've done some rafting on the Colorado, and I thought I'd try my hand at fishing in Alaska. That's something I never had a chance to do.'

'Did you have any luck?'

'Fantastic!' he said, and promptly changed the subject. 'Did your folks go with you on the Float Trip?' He wondered how difficult it was going to be to get her alone. She saw his look sharpen and wondered why he would be curious about that. Maybe he wasn't. He had a way of looking intense about things that certainly didn't seem to have much importance.

'My father did,' she told him, 'but Mother begged off. It's just as well. It was so rough! They told us the turbulence of the air was very unusual, but then, this many sunny days is something unusual too. We certainly got our money's worth on that ride.'

She wondered if he would ask her if Irish had accompanied them, but before he could say more the subject of her thoughts bounded

111

into view, all exuberance and incredible good looks. He's just a gorgeous, healthy animal, she thought as Irish strode toward them, but I'm beginning to think his bark is worse than his bite. He hasn't made a serious pass yet, even though he comes on so strong. Was he just all bluff? And what would she do if he weren't?

For the first time since her divorce she found herself taking a serious interest in a man. Take it easy, my girl, she warned herself. This is just a cruise. One of those here-today-gone-tomorrow liaisons ... And what you are experiencing right now is just the old red corpuscles bouncing around, responding to all the macho exterior. They woke up when you first bumped into Werner, too, remember? And now you're beginning to find him too uptight and just a little dull. The trouble is they've just been asleep too long! She grinned to herself at the foolishness of her mental imagery and Irish, now lounging at the rail in front of her, felt his heart turn over as she looked up at him with that silly little smile.

Steady, old boy, he told himself. This job you're on is going to be ticklish enough. Don't make it any harder than you have to. You can't afford to have feelings for these people right now, one way or the other.

Leonie said suddenly, 'Oh, look, here come those nice Carrascos I mentioned yesterday.

They're from Mexico City. She can barely build a sentence in English, but with that smile and those eyes she doesn't have to. Isn't she a doll? It still startles me to see a Mexican with big blue eyes. He's a lawyer, and she was a nurse before they married. Their first names are Luis and Maribel, but I don't know if it would be proper to use them as we do with everyone else we've met. They seem to be a little more formal than we *gringos* are.'

'You seem to know a lot about them,' the judge said, 'When did you meet?'

'We had a lovely visit in the early morning coffee line when I got up there ahead of you yesterday. I took to them right away.' She turned to the newcomers, a handsome couple in their mid-thirties. 'Hello, there! It's so good to see you again. I'd like you to meet my parents.'

Introductions were made all around, while Maribel Carrasco stood, uncomprehending, smiling her shy sweet smile. Her face brightened with interest as her husband explained to her in Spanish that John Warwick was a federal judge. '*¿Un juez?! Que interesanté!*' She added something else in rapid Spanish as she threw Luis a surprisingly mischievous look. He laughed and turned to the judge. 'My wife says, if you will permit me to say, that you are a very handsome man, and that when I am older and more distinguished—perhaps a judge as well—that

113

she hopes I look exactly like you! I hope the personal remark does not offend you.'

'I am never offended by a compliment from a beautiful woman!' John assured him bowing to Maribel with oldtime gallantry. 'I'm flattered.'

Maribel, realizing her husband had translated her observation, flushed most becomingly, reproaching him gently with her lovely eyes. But it was obvious she adored him. Her gaze seldom left his face. Leonie, watching the elegant woman, thought her look held a flicker of pain or sadness. For a fleeting moment she wondered why, but the Carrascos moved on, and their little group was immediately caught up in a brisk discussion of their rehearsal for the Talent Show.

'Now that we're alone again,' Sanna said, 'I want to tell you my inspiration.' She had lowered her voice because the acts were supposed to be kept secret until the night of the performance. 'I thought we'd give each character a musical theme. Werner will be doing the reading, and he can stand close to the piano and give me the cues. For example, at the beginning I thought I'd start with the "Maple Leaf Rag" when the piano player is doing what the poem calls a "rag-time tune." Then, when it says, "Back of the bar, in a solo game, sat Dangerous Dan McGrew," I'll use the 'William Tell Overture'. You know,' she explained to the nonmusical part of her audience. 'Da-da-dum, da-da-dum, da-da-dum-dum-dum. The theme of the Lone Ranger. Just a few bars, and then I'll stop when he starts reading again. His next line is, "And watching his luck was his light-of-love, the lady that's known as Lou." I thought I'd use "Bird in a Gilded Cage" there. Then every time each character is mentioned I can use his or her identifying theme. What do you think?'

'I think it's a marvelous idea, Mom,' Leonie said with enthusiasm. 'What other selections did you pick?'

'I'm not sure yet,' Sanna admitted. 'I'll want something special for "the stranger." He's really the most dramatic character. Nobody knows who he is, but you're beginning to suspect he's the man who was spurned by Lou because he hadn't struck it rich yet when she took up with Dangerous Dan, who had.'

'Hey!' Irish said suddenly. 'That reminds me. Wait until you see what I found in Juneau—the perfect disguise for 'the stranger.' They'll never recognize you, Judge! I looked all over for a false beard, but couldn't find one. Then, in a small variety store, I found this. I brought it to show you.' He pulled out a piece of fur from his pocket. 'I was in luck,' he said. 'This was the only brown one. All the others were white.'

'What kind of animal comes in an assortment of colors?' Leonie asked.

'It's a rabbit pelt,' Irish told them. 'It's not quite the right shape, but it will be easy enough to trim it to look like a full beard. I scrounged a beat-up old fishing cap from one of the crew. It's just a soft cap with a bill, but has big earflaps, and I thought if we could pin the rabbit-fur beard to it, the stranger's face really would be "most hair," as the poem says.'

'That's great!' Leonie exclaimed. 'What other props will we need? Will we be able to get them all? The ship's supply of costumes and such is very limited.'

'Well, the guns, of course,' Irish responded. 'I had good luck with those in Juneau too. I even found some caps that would make a loud enough noise to sound authentic. They'll be much better than our original idea of popping paper bags for sound effects. And you won't have to worry about somebody else missing their cue. The judge and I will just fire away at each other when it's time. Tell you what. Let's try to find one of the smaller, unoccupied lounges, and we'll have our rehearsal there tonight after Glacier Bay. I know one that has a piano, and nobody can see or hear us with the door closed, so we won't give our skit away. The Main Lounge is almost always occupied since the bar's right there.'

'That's a good idea,' Sanna agreed. 'If you'll direct me, I think I'll go in now and try out the piano. It will be some time before the glaciers come into view.'

There were two entrances, one at either end of the rectangular-shaped lounge. After Sanna had satisfied herself that she could remember the old songs well enough to play them from memory, she sank into one of the big lounge chairs to note them in order on her copy of the poem.

She gave a little sigh of contentment. How perfect to relax like this in a peaceful corner. What more could one want? Her daughter was showing signs of recovering from the traumatic experience that had almost shattered her. Her hard-working husband was getting a much-needed rest. Thank goodness he'd suffered no ill effects from that raft trip. What a foolish thing for a man his age! But then, he'd had a marvelous time.

She sighed again, this time with anxiety. Did one simply try to live as long as one could, regardless of the quality of life, or did one die happy? There was something to be said for John's point of view. To give up everything one enjoyed would make life an empty shell, a drag. But there was much to be said for some commonsensical precautions too. After all, the doctor had suggested he relax completely after the strain he'd been under, even though his heart problem didn't appear to be serious. Why were men such hardheaded creatures?

The sound of an opening door distracted her and she peeked around the sides of the big chair to see Luis and Maribel Carrasco enter the small lounge.

Luis's low voice was coaxing, soothing, a tone one uses with a distraught child. And Maribel was certainly distraught. Tears rolled down her sculptured cheeks, and her exquisite hands turned and intertwined as she spoke. It was obvious they were seeking an isolated place to resolve a problem and believed the small room to be deserted.

Sanna had the uncomfortable feeling of eavesdropping on a private conversation, but there was no way she could exit without announcing her presence. They were, of course, speaking in Spanish, and since she could not understand one word, she decided to stay. To show herself now would be extremely embarrassing for them.

They were not quarreling. That would have been surprising. They were so exceptionally devoted and affectionate with one another that everyone called them the honeymoon couple, though it was generally known they'd been married for years. But Maribel was terribly upset about something, and Luis displayed the typical male helplessness in the face of feminine tears.

'No, no, no, *mi amor*,' he crooned. *'No*

118

llores. No llores, mi vida.' But it did no good to beg her not to cry, for her tears came faster and her sobs grew more heartrending. Luis's sensitive face reflected every one of her sobs like a physical pain from a blow.

Sanna could have cried for the anguish in their voices and wished herself anywhere but where she was. She curled herself tighter behind the concealing wings of the big chair.

What could have happened? Bad news from home? She understood they had no children. Whatever the problem, it was plainly no small matter.

She was still very much upset after Luis, unable to calm his wife, managed to convince her to go to their cabin to rest a while.

CHAPTER TWELVE

INTERPOLATE...
to insert or introduce between other things.

As they climbed a steep railed set of metal steps to the boat deck John Warwick said, 'I understand the Park Rangers from Glacier Bay National Monument came on board at 6.00 this morning and will be with us all day to lecture and answer questions. I wonder where they came from.'

'I can tell you that,' Sanna informed him.

119

'They're stationed at Bartlett Cove, at the head of Glacier Bay. Perhaps we can find one before they're mobbed with questions.'

They found their Ranger, an attractive young woman. At the same time, excited shouts were heard from the foredeck rail. '*Look!*' It was a chorus from many throats, closely akin to the '*Aaaah!*' heard at a fireworks display.

A whooshing jet of air and water shot fifteen feet high as they watched. Then another. And another. Then a huge body arched and plunged smoothly back into the sea. At the last moment an enormous tail fluke flipped up into a gigantic T as the creature vanished into the water.

'What was *that!*' Leonie could hardly speak for excitement.

'Those are humpback whales,' the smiling Ranger informed her. 'You're really lucky to see them today. They're getting scarcer by the minute.'

'They're an endangered species, then?' Sanna asked.

'Desperately. And we really know very little about them, in spite of all our study and research. There used to be many thousands of them, but they've been so slaughtered there are only a few animals left to study.'

'Are they here only in the summer or do they stay year round?' the judge asked.

'There is one small group of humpbacks

that seems to spend the winter in Alaska. We're not sure why, but they're the nonconformists. Most of them move to subtropical breeding grounds in the winter and live off their body fat after eating all summer long.'

'I'm curious to know how long it takes them to get back,' Leonie said.

'About two months. They generally enter the Gulf of Alaska in April.'

'Do you suppose we'll see them again,' John asked, 'or are they gone for good?'

'Well, normally they'll stay down for ten to twenty minutes. But they can stay underwater for forty-five. We'll just have to wait and see.'

They did not see the whales again, but were thrilled with even the brief sighting. It was interesting to learn from the Park Ranger that the fluke, or flipper, of each whale was as unique as a human's fingerprints. Each had its own color, shape, and marking.

The brief flurry of excitement subsided and they settled into their observation posts, delighted to see that Dr. Barnes was already there.

'Oho!' John teased him. 'You're in for it now. Do you want to leave while you have the chance, or can you put up with questions from three Warwicks at once?'

'I can't think of anything nicer,' Morton Barnes said, his eyes twinkling as he smiled down from his great height. 'What do you

121

want to know? You're the ones at risk, you know. Anyone brave enough to *ask* me to expound on glaciers simply must suffer the consequences. I never seem to get tired of talking about them. I'm sure I tell most people far more than they want to know.'

'Well, that's not the case here,' Leonie assured him. 'We're all simply fascinated by your "rivers of ice," and I, for one, want to know all about them. Why don't you just start out, and we can ask specific questions as they occur. Fair enough?'

'Fair enough.' The keen gray eyes that belied his 'absent-minded-professor' look warmed as he made no attempt to hide his pleasure in talking to such a lovely young woman.

'In the first place,' he began. 'when Captain George Vancouver came through here in 1794 this looked like just a minor inlet with a towering wall of ice, and Glacier Bay as it is now did not exist. But glaciers don't stand still. They advance and retreat. For example, Muir Glacier receded about five miles in seven years, but the snouts of Grand Pacific and Johns Hopkins have moved forward gradually.'

'How many glaciers will we see?' Sanna asked.

Barnes replied, 'Not many of the tributary glaciers that once supplied the huge ice sheet still extend to the sea, but in the 4,400 square miles of Glacier Bay National Monument you'll see sixteen active tidewater glaciers.'

'How close will we get?' Leonie wanted to know. 'We're all dying to get pictures.'

'Well, that depends upon how active the glacier is. You'll probably have an opportunity to see a spectacular show of geologic forces in action, and that can be dangerous. As the water undermines the ice fronts, great blocks of ice, up to 200 feet high, break loose and crash into the sea, creating huge waves and filling the narrow inlets with massive icebergs. We call this "calving." Muir and Johns Hopkins Glaciers discharge such great volumes of ice that it's seldom possible to come closer to their cliffs than two miles or so. Floating ice is a hazard too. But we should be able to get within a half mile of Margerie Glacier. It's very active, too, but it's more accessible. With some luck you should see some calving of the icebergs.'

'What a funny term!' Sanna wrinkled her nose in amusement. 'I can't see any connection between the birth of a warm, soft little calf and a chunk of ice!'

Leonie said, 'Margerie is the glacier pictured on the posters and postcards we have. Was it named for someone's wife or daughter?'

'No,' Dr. Barnes smiled. 'The name is Margerie,'—he spelled it—'not Marjorie. And it was named after a French glaciologist.'

123

'Now I have a question,' John said, 'and it may sound very silly to you, but I have never been able to figure out how a huge chunk of ice can be light enough to float in the first place.'

'No question is silly,' Morton Barnes reminded him tactfully before answering. 'We can't all be informed on the same things. I always thought a tort was something to eat, but I understand you deal with them in your business, Judge.'

'You'd have to put an 'e' on them, Dr. Barnes,' he laughed, 'or they'd be indigestible.'

Sanna added, laughing, 'Tortes are more fattening, too!'

'But there's a simple explanation for your question,' Barnes continued. 'In an iceberg there is more space between the molecules of water than in liquid form. So ice will then be lighter and able to float.'

'I really don't understand what makes a glacier anyway,' Leonie confessed. 'Would it take too long to explain?'

'Oh, no, not at all,' the professor said. 'It's really very simple. Glaciers form because the snow that falls each year in the high mountains does not all melt, but accumulates and is turned into ice. Newfallen snow changes first into granular snow consisting of round grains of ice. As the depth increases, these ice grains become more closely packed

124

and in time fuse into solid ice. When there is sufficient thickness, volume, and weight, it flows down into lower regions to a point where the rate of melting equals the rate of accumulation. That point is the terminus, or snout, of the glacier. Then, when...' He interrupted himself with a softly breathed 'Aaah! Here we are.' His tone was almost reverent.

They had all been so engrossed in his explanation they had forgotten to watch for the appearance of Margerie Glacier. Now the reaction was universal: *'Oh!'*

No postcard, no painting, no brochure hyperbole could do justice to the beauty of a glacier seen with the human eye. There was a long moment's hush. Then Sanna, spellbound, breathed, 'Did you ever see anything so beautiful!'

'Impressive, isn't it?' Dr. Barnes' lowered voice reflected everyone's feeling at the awe-inspiring sight. 'I never tire of looking at that incredible beauty. It's one place where the word "unique" actually fits.'

'It's very humbling,' the judge observed. 'Especially when you consider how long this has all been standing here while we humans come and go.'

They were all silent again, gripped by the same awareness of timelessness and cosmic forces that comes to those fortunate enough to commune with towering mountains and restless oceans. They watched the incredible rivers of blue-white ice, hundreds of feet thick, flowing stonily to the sea. It was a rare and moving experience.

Dr. Barnes broke the silence. 'And these are relative newcomers, remnants of a general ice advance which began about 4,000 years ago. It doesn't begin to compare with the continental glaciation of earlier Pleistocene times.'

The judge said thoughtfully, 'A sight like this does tend to make you wish you could retreat to a more uncomplicated time when other natural beauties were as unspoiled as this.'

Leonie spoke. 'I didn't realize until we saw the movie on Alaska how quickly everything changed even up here. How fortunate that this was made a national monument so it couldn't be desecrated.'

Her father agreed. 'Yes. Did you know, some of the fiercest fighting of the Pacific took place here on American soil. When the Japanese took the outlying islands during World War II and threatened to invade the mainland, things speeded up in a hurry. Alaska got bridges and roads super-fast. It's incredible to think that the 1600-mile Alaskan Highway was built by 16,000 men in only eight months. And, of course, once oil was found, things were never the same again.'

'You mean we now have Eskimos pulling

their sleds with snowmobiles instead of dogs?'
Leonie laughed.

A sudden shout went up as a rumble, then a roar was heard, and an iceberg bigger than a house cracked loose from the massive glacier walls to splash mightily into the water. The boat rocked gently as the swells reached them.

'Oh, no,' Leonie wailed. 'It all happened so fast I couldn't get a picture. But wasn't that exciting! At least I did get to see an iceberg calve.'

'And the whales,' Sanna reminded her.

Barnes pricked up his ears. 'Oh, did you get to see the humpbacks? That's getting to be a rarer and rarer sight.'

'So our young Park Ranger told us,' Sanna said. 'Apparently they have decreased drastically in numbers.'

'Indeed they have.' The professor shook his long, lean head mournfully. 'There used to be twenty to twenty-four that usually fed in this area, but back in 1979 while the usual whale population arrived on time, when they left in mid-July the second group never showed up. The National Park Service has restricted the number of cruise ships in an attempt to protect them.

'Needless to say, it's created quite a controversy between them and the visitor industry. As usual, there are two sides to the problem. The visitor-related businesses claim there are other factors besides the underwater noise from the skyrocketing number of visitors to the area. And while the national parks were created with visitor use in mind, the mandate says they are to be maintained in their natural state. The Superintendent of Glacier Bay maintains that in a sense these parks are living museums and, of course, he's right.' He broke off, exclaiming, 'Look! There are some harbor seals. Not as dramatic as your whales, but they are interesting.'

There was a flurry of activity as cameras were levelled and pictures taken of the sleek brown animals on the ice floes. Barnes informed them that the seals 'pup' on the icebergs to give their young protection from predators such as bears, wolves and wolverines.

Werner Heinsohn and Irish approached. The big Irishman was booming his deep-chested laugh and even Heinsohn was chuckling.

Leonie's raised eyebrows questioned their hilarity as she made room for them at the railing.

Irish laughed again and said, 'You know Mrs. Evans, whose cabin is next to the Beardsleys? She's Canadian, you know, and sometimes she has trouble with American expressions. You can always get in trouble with a foreign language,' he grinned. 'Her alarm clock wasn't working, and she asked

Charlie Beardsley if he'd knock on her door so she could get up early enough to see the glaciers today. Just now I heard her thanking Mrs. Beardsley. She said, "I appreciate so much your husband knocking me up at 5:30.'"

As they all joined in the laughter, the subject of the levity approached. 'Howdy!' There was no need to turn around. The accent was unmistakable.

'Hi, Charlie! We were just talking about you.' Leonie really liked the Beardsleys, and found Charlie immensely entertaining, whether he meant to be or not.

'What did you all think of them icebergs in the makin'?' Charlie asked. 'Wish I had one of my guns here.' His bright eyes were more prominent than ever in his amazement.

'A gun!' Leonie was horrified. 'For what?'

'Don't fret yourself, little lady,' Charlie reassured her. 'I wasn't fixin' to shoot me one of them pretty little animals. I just wanted to start another fall of ice.'

'Sorry, Charlie,' Barnes said in a lugubrious voice, and they all laughed at his chance to use the line from the famous tuna commercial. 'There's really nothing you can do to hurry things up. Shots, blowing horns, yells—nothing works. They simply come when they're ready. Like other births.'

As people rushed from one side of the ship to the other as glacier after glacier came into view, the initial excitement dimmed a little, but the awe was still there. It was impossible to be unmoved by the magnificent sight.

Leonie suddenly noticed that Heinsohn and Irish were engrossed in a low-toned conversation, and wondered what they could be discussing that would take their attention from the glaciers.

It was well for her peace of mind and her enjoyment of the dramatic and hauntingly beautiful sights of the rest of the day that she could not know.

CHAPTER THIRTEEN

PROCRASTINATE...
to postpone until a future time.

The next day dawned cool and misty, but there were no complaints because it was to be a full day at sea. The Warwicks, lined up for early morning coffee, commented once more on their good luck in having had such incredibly fine weather to date, especially in Glacier Bay.

'No matter how long I live or how many exotic places I see,' Leonie said, 'I'll never forget the beauty of that place. Those calm inlets like blue glass, the snow-topped mountains around them, and then those marvelous ice-rivers inching down to the water, were nothing less than a soul-satisfying experience. I can't tell you how grateful I am to both of you for talking me into this trip. If you had told me just a week ago I would be feeling this good and enjoying myself so much I would have laughed at the idea.'

'You look just great too, Lee,' her father said, his voice husky with emotion.

Leonie noticed his use of the diminutive name, something he did only when he was either teasing or very serious, never in between. She had an odd feeling of accomplishment as though some tremendous milestone had been passed. Maybe it had. She too was aware of the change in herself. What troubled her was the thought it might be only temporary: not only the magic of the cruise and the overwhelming beauties of nature they had experienced, but also the encounter with a fascinating man in a highly romantic setting.

Along with the heightened awareness a trip of this kind fostered, there was also a heightening of emotions. Perhaps it was because of the isolation from the everyday world a tour group feels, as well as the daily proximity of the other passengers. Would she feel the same strong attraction to Irish if they had met in her home town? She wondered if she were being too careful, too fearful of Irish's ability to penetrate her fiercely-held

131

defenses.

She had always assumed she would find the same love and support in her own husband that Sanna had in her father. It troubled her to think that the trauma of her dreadful miscalculation in choosing Walter as a mate might have wounded her so deeply she could never allow herself to love again.

Irish, mounting the stairs to the Prom Deck in search of Leonie, was tormented by similar thoughts. Why, he asked himself unhappily, couldn't I have met this girl some other time, some other place? Falling in love was the very last thing he'd anticipated when he'd embarked on this masquerade. And he was certain Leonie was beginning to return his feeling, in spite of her careful control. He could see it in her eyes.

He thought suddenly of a line from Margaret Mitchell's 'Gone With the Wind,' describing Scarlett O'Hara. 'Her manners,' the book declared, 'had been imposed upon her; her eyes were her own.' So it was with Leonie's cool friendliness, warring with the intensity of her unguarded glances. What an intoxicating combination! And Scarlett, Mitchell noted, while extremely charming, was not beautiful. Leonie was exquisite.

As he reached the little family group, his heart leapt at the sudden brief flash of fire in Leonie's lambent green eyes before she controlled her expression.

'May I join you?' he asked. 'I promise not to speak if no one is awake yet at this unholy hour. I know I can ambulate for hours before my brain joins the rest of me.'

'I want to speak to you,' Sanna declared. 'I heard just a tantalizing snippet of a conversation you were having with Dr. Barnes yesterday. I've been dying to ask you about it.'

'What were we discussing?' Irish cocked a quizzical eyebrow. 'With Dr. Barnes it might be anything.' He shook his head in wonderment. 'That man is a walking encyclopedia!'

'He had made some remark about "Southeast Sneakers,"' Sanna said, 'and when you questioned him he laughed and said you needed to learn the native language. I didn't hear what followed.'

'Oh, yes, I remember that one,' Irish laughed. 'That was a most interesting conversation.'

'Every region seems to have its own vocabulary,' John said. 'It certainly would be fun to learn this one. Would you care to educate us?'

'With pleasure. In the first place, when an Alaskan goes "Outside," he's not necessarily merely going outdoors. It means he's "going south," as they say, to the Lower 48. But, if he did go outdoors he'd need his "Southeast Sneakers," which is what they call rubber boots. He himself would be a native—spelled two ways. With a capital "N" it refers to the original people who lived in the state. Most Natives in this area are Tlingit, Haida or Simshian. If you're a native with a lower case "n," it simply means you were born here.'

'They certainly love to tease the visitors here,' Leonie added. 'I heard Dr. Barnes say you can distinguish the visitors from the residents on sunny days when you see the latter crossing the street several times in order to keep walking in the sun! With which,' she added, 'we've certainly been blessed to date.'

'That's because I came along!' Charlie Beardsley declared as he came up in time to hear the last of the conversation. 'That's all you good folks needed—a Texan on the trip.' His infectious grin, splitting a ruddy moon face, topped by sparse gray hair, made him look something like a jovial pumpkin. Leonie, who had a sudden insane desire to blacken his front teeth to heighten the effect, choked back a giggle and said hastily, 'Mr. Beardsley, I heard you had a story to tell.'

'Please call me Charlie, ma'am,' he begged, his face redder than usual. Leonie half expected him to turn his big toe on the deck and say 'Aw, shucks!'

'Okay,' she smiled at him. 'Charlie it is.'

He hesitated a moment, casting an uncertain glance at the elegant Warwick women. 'Well, actually, ma'am, I was thinking only of the menfolks. It's just a mite ... well, you know...' Then, to Leonie's delight, he actually did say it. 'Aw, shucks! I can't see you good ladies getting all bent out of shape over a little joke. So here goes.

'It seems that in the old days,' Charlie began, 'a sourdough was someone who had seen an Alaskan winter through from beginning to end. Then, when the tenderfeet came up from the Lower 48 they started a new version. Two of the requirements were to fight a bear and spend a night with an Eskimo woman.

'This was all carefully explained to one not-so-bright Cheechako and he said, in effect, "Sure, I can handle all that." Well, they waited and waited for him to come back, wondering what could have happened to him. Finally he showed up, in a terrible state. He was black and blue, scratched all over, with his clothes hanging on him in rags. When they questioned him he said, "Well, that was a little rough, but I made it. Now, when do I get to fight with an Eskimo?"'

It was so outrageous even Sanna had to laugh, although she was usually cool to anything of an off-color nature. And although Charlie might be a little earthy, he was not a vulgar man. She waved a slender hand and said, 'I think I'll leave before things go from bad to worse.'

Charlie flushed crimson. 'I hope I didn't

offend you, Mrs. Warwick,' he said. He looked about to cry.

'Not at all,' Sanna assured him, smiling. 'I'm teasing. I really do have to leave because I have an appointment at the beauty shop. See y'all later.' Her wicked imitation of Charlie's drawl brought a fresh tide of red but a big smile and a look of admiration to his good-natured face. He blew her a kiss and she winked at him.

'That's quite a lady,' he declared, watching her graceful departure with obvious pleasure, ignoring his dumpy little wife's disapproving scowl.

'If we're going to deal with irreverent subjects,' John said, 'I'll tell you about something I came across in my reading that interested me. The ship's library has a wealth of material. This is not too high-class a subject, to be sure, but interesting nevertheless.

'One thing that puzzled me was what in the world they would do about sanitation in a land where ground in many areas remained permanently frozen. So I researched, and found that engineers still have a problem making waste and water flow when it's fifty below. But I learned that they have pipes carry hot water or steam alongside the water and sewage mains. Of course, in many areas outhouses are still being used. It was amusing to learn of the ingenious methods invented to

136

increase the comfort of the situation.

'Some had carved styrofoam seat covers. Some would slip wool socks over each side of a split toilet seat. One considerate host even put heating cables inside the sock and would preheat them a few minutes before his guests went outside. And, apparently, it was routine for many to keep the seat behind the stove, ready to be grabbed as needed.'

He stopped, a little embarrassed, then relaxed in the wake of hearty laughter that followed.

As they laughed, Leonie thought about the universality of the human condition: the pressing bladder, the empty belly, the aching head. People were people, whether their background was the frozen tundra, the soaring mountains or the scorching desert. And it was probably just as well not to take it all too seriously. Those who seemed to survive best appeared to be those who could look at life—and themselves—with a wry sense of humor. She thought, I wonder if perhaps that's been part of my problem. I really have been pretty sheltered. I'm going to have to learn to accept life on its own terms: to roll with the punches, as they say.

The beauty shop was in the bowels of the ship, next to the theatre. Small, of course, and compact, limited as to supplies. There were two operators, two shampoo basins. A young black woman was being shampooed, and the other customer was under a dryer. She was an elderly dowager type, dripping diamonds and gold chains, all constantly fingered by her exquisitely manicured fingers. Why, Sanna thought, you'd think we were making a crossing on the old Queen Elizabeth!

The motion of the ship was considerably more noticeable on this level and the Duchess, as Sanna immediately thought of her, had a chair with a short leg. It had, of course, immediately become a rocking chair, and Sanna watched the poor lady become greener by the minute, completely abandoning her air of haughty superiority. It seemed obvious she had stuffed a well-endowed figure into a highly constricting girdle, and Sanna spent an uneasy few moments hoping the woman would get dry and combed out before she got sick.

As the dryer clicked off, Sanna thought: maybe it will help if I make conversation, to take her mind off her problems. If she'll speak to me, that is. She did look so very superior.

As the older woman settled in the chair for her comb-out she had to face Sanna directly in the cramped quarters. Sanna smiled and introduced herself. The Duchess at first frowned and directed what seemed a supercilious look at Sanna, then she smiled unexpectedly and said, 'Just a moment, my dear. Let me get my glasses so I can get a proper look at you.' The operator handed them to her, and there was an immediate transformation. The apparently haughty, distant *grande dame* magically became a warm and talkative woman.

Why, poor dear, Sanna thought, she can't see an inch in front of her nose without those things! With everything a blur, she doesn't dare risk misreading people's expressions. With her glasses on, the elderly woman's seasickness seemed to diminish considerably too. She fell into a lively discussion with Sanna concerning the ship, passengers she had met, and the marvelous sights they had seen. As they talked, a picture emerged of a very lonely old lady who had a great deal of money and not much else. Her husband, she told Sanna, had been with the State Department, and they had lived for many years in Buenos Aires. They had no children, and after his death she had simply drifted from one trip or cruise to the other, seeking companionship, spending as little time as possible between tours in her luxury condominium. Sanna found her very likable and a little pathetic.

In the middle of a comparison of their reactions to Glacier Bay, Maribel Carrasco came in to keep an appointment. Sanna was surprised to see her alone. Where was Luis? And how could she make her wishes known

139

without speaking English?

Maribel's dazzling smile illuminated her lovely face and her eyes lit up immediately when she recognized Sanna. '*Buenos dias,* Señora Wahrweek.'

'Good morning, Maribel.' Sanna was as delighted to see her, but the two women could only smile at each other in embarrassment and frustration because they could not communicate further. But Maribel had apparently had some coaching from Luis. She turned to the operator and said haltingly, 'I ... need ... mmm ... the hair cleaned and ... hmm ... so.' There was much gesturing and pantomiming with aristocratic hands to indicate what hairstyle was desired.

'Do you want conditioner, too?' asked the operator.

Maribel looked utterly blank until, to her delight and astonishment, Mrs. Courtland, the Duchess, broke into a spate of rapid-fire Spanish. After the operator was made to understand what was wanted, Maribel and Mrs. Courtland embarked upon an animated conversation.

'How marvelous that she could find someone like you to talk with,' Sanna said, when there was a lull. 'I'm certainly no help there. It must be very lonely for her on this trip with only her husband to talk to.'

'Not any more,' Mrs. Courtland said stoutly. 'We shall soon remedy that! And what a lovely thing she is. Frankly, I'm delighted at the opportunity to speak Spanish again. It's frightening how soon one loses a language that's not used, no matter how well known.'

'Ask her if her husband is all right,' Sanna urged. 'I can't believe he'd let her come here alone unless he's under the weather. He speaks excellent English.'

Mrs. Courtland interrogated Maribel briefly, then informed Sanna, 'I'm afraid you're right. He's quite seasick. Apparently he's not too well anyway, but she seems reluctant to talk about that.'

Sanna, remembering the incident in the lounge the night before, thought: well, it would undoubtedly be good for Maribel to unburden herself to such a sympathetic soul.

She left them chatting happily away as she proceeded with her own beautification.

CHAPTER FOURTEEN

IMPLICATE...
to involve intimately or incriminatingly.

Scurry was not a word Sanna would have thought to apply to Mrs. Courtland, but there she was, scurrying down the Prom Deck just as fast as dignity and Spandex would permit.

'Oh, my dear,' she gasped as she reached Sanna. 'I must talk to you!'

In spite of her concern Sanna thought irreverently: if she doesn't get out of that fool corset she's going to have a stroke! I'll bet she needs a can opener to get undressed at night. 'What's wrong?' she asked the obviously agitated woman.

'With me, nothing,' the Duchess replied. 'It's Maribel. Or rather, her husband.'

'Is Luis worse?' Sanna asked, alarmed.

'We can't talk here,' the Duchess declared. 'Let's find a more private place. How about that small lounge with the piano?' She looked around her as furtively as if she were divulging state secrets, then led a thoroughly mystified Sanna away.

The little-used lounge was empty. As they positioned themselves with chairs close together, Sanna was reminded once more of the previous evening when she had inadvertently been a party to the Carrascos' private conversation. Perhaps there was a connection between the tearful scene and Mrs. Courtland's soon-to-be-divulged secret. She waited expectantly.

'Poor Maribel! Oh, poor darling!' Unexpectedly, tears sprang to the elderly lady's eyes as Sanna stared at her, astonished. It was the last thing she expected from the Duchess.

'What is it?' she asked anxiously,

thoroughly alarmed now. This seemed to be a problem far more serious than a seasick husband.

It was. Mrs. Courtland wrung her hands in anguish and wailed, 'Oh, my dear, it's Luis. And they are so completely devoted to each other. In fact, that's the problem. You see, he's dying!'

'*What!*' Sanna was stunned by the blunt announcement. 'Are you *sure?*' Luis? Handsome, robust-looking Luis *dying?*

'I'm afraid so. It's leukemia. Poor Maribel is devastated, of course. It must be hellish to know the end is coming soon for someone you love and be helpless to avert it. And until now there hasn't been a soul to whom she could unburden herself.' The tears came again and she blotted them fiercely, determined not to lose control again. 'At least with my George I had the consolation of a long and wonderfully happy life together. But they are too *young* for this!'

Another breakdown seemed imminent, and Sanna hastened to keep her talking. 'She told you all about it, then?'

'Yes. You see, even though he still looks quite well, he has only a short time to live. They thought this cruise would be a distraction, rather than sitting around at home, waiting for the end. It's something they've always wanted to do anyway. They have no children. Most of the time he feels

143

pretty well, but when he has these sick spells poor Maribel just falls apart, fearful he's going to die even sooner than expected. It's so unfair!' She sounded utterly sad, but the tears were held at bay now. 'Oh, I wish we could help them some way. At least she can talk to me, poor darling. She hasn't even had that release up until now. She simply poured her heart out to me a while ago, after we left the beauty shop.'

Sanna had an inspiration. 'I know! We'll involve them in our play! We've had such fun with it. And if that's not a distraction, I don't know what would be. Maybe he'll feel well enough to participate in the rehearsal. There's not a great deal of action involved, actually, even though it's all very dramatic.'

'But, my dear, you're forgetting. Maribel barely has a half dozen words in English.'

'No, I wasn't forgetting that,' Sanna assured her. 'But I did forget to tell you what we're doing. It's a rendition of Robert W. Service's famous poem, "The Shooting of Dan McGrew." Someone will read the poem while the rest of us act it out. There are no lines to speak at all. In fact, Luis could even be "Dangerous Dan" himself. All he'd have to do is sit at the table and pretend to play cards. One of the young men, the one they call Irish, was supposed to have that part, but he can do the reading. He has a beautiful speaking voice. I just found out that Werner

144

Heinsohn, the other young man, won't be able to participate, so there will be a part available. Do you know the poem?'

'I'm afraid not.'

'Well,' Sanna continued, seeing she had the older woman's attention, and trying to convince her that they could help, 'there's "Dangerous Dan McGrew" and his girl friend, "Lou." My daughter Leonie will have that part. Then there's "the stranger," played by my husband, and assorted poker players. I'm the piano player. The setting is an old-time saloon in the gold rush days. Maribel can be the barmaid. She won't have to say a single word, just smile and look beautiful, which is natural for her. What do you think?'

'Well, I don't know,' Mrs. Courtland began doubtfully. But by the time they finished talking they had agreed it would be worth a try. 'We'll see what the rest have to say about it,' Sanna suggested.

To their immense satisfaction Luis was taken with the idea immediately. He had improved greatly during the afternoon and joined them for dinner.

'But that's marvelous!' he exclaimed. '*Fantástico!* We shall amuse ourselves greatly.' He turned to Maribel, speaking staccato Spanish. She looked at him adoringly, but seemed uncertain. Then she said something to him softly.

'My wife is a little unsure of the plan

145

because I was unwell earlier today. But that was only the motion of the ship,' he lied gallantly, 'and I took my medicine and am quite recovered now. You say the rehearsal is tonight?'

'Yes,' Leonie told him. 'Each of us will have a copy of the poem. They have a copying machine in the library. All you have to do is follow the cues of the reader.'

Luis looked puzzled. 'What is this word, "cue?"'

Mrs. Courtland, who had scarcely let Maribel out of her sight since that morning, came to the rescue. *'Es un señal, Luis, un indicio,'* she informed him.

'Ah!' His face cleared. 'So all I must do is to put on the costume and do what the reader indicates, no?'

'That's all there is to it,' Leonie assured him. 'But you won't even have to do that much.' She turned to her mother. 'He'll have to be one of the poker players, won't he, with all the other parts filled?'

'Actually,' Sanna said, 'I thought we'd let him do the part of "Dan McGrew." Werner Heinsohn's backed out, you know, and Irish would do an excellent job as the narrator with that gorgeous voice of his.' She tried to give Leonie a meaningful look willing her agreement, for she felt certain Luis would get more caught up in the spirit of the thing if he had a major role.

146

But Leonie only picked up on part of the message. 'You say Werner's dropped out? Why?'

'You'll have to ask him that,' Sanna replied, then turned back to Luis. 'I'll get your copy of the poem to you right after dinner. The Talent Show is to be held after our tour of Anchorage.'

They finished their dinner on a note of high anticipation, and Maribel was visibly cheered at her husband's show of interest in the project. He seemed quite elated at the prospect.

Leonie hunted up Werner Heinsohn at the first opportunity.

'What's this about your leaving the Great Performance?' she demanded. 'Aren't you coming to the rehearsal tonight?'

'I'm sorry, Leonie,' the big blond said, looking discomfited. 'I'll have to back out. I thought you knew. I told your mother.'

'She just mentioned it now. I certainly was surprised. What happened? Did you just change your mind? I thought you were enjoying it as much as the rest of us.' But even as she spoke she wondered at herself, for she realized with a start that she really didn't care. Heinsohn's presence was no longer important to her. She kept her face expressionless as she waited for his answer.

'Oh, I certainly was enjoying it.' He hesitated. It really must seem inexplicable to

147

her. Better to tell part of the truth. That was always safest. Why lie, when you merely had to evade?

'It didn't seem necessary to mention it, but actually I have some business in Homer tomorrow afternoon,' he said, 'and if I get held up and don't get back in time for the sailing, it would leave all of you in the lurch at the last minute.'

'Not make the sailing?' Leonie was bewildered. 'How could you possibly miss the sailing?'

'Oh, that's no big deal,' Heinsohn answered. 'I could always rent a car and catch up with the rest of you in Anchorage. I'm just not sure how long my business will take.'

'But the Talent Show isn't until the day after tomorrow,' Leonie protested. 'And you really don't need to practice when you just have to read.' She suppressed a little voice within her that insisted on saying, 'Come on, now, Leonie. You know you wouldn't give a hoot except that you want to perform with an arm around Irish, not Luis Carrasco.' She didn't think it necessary to inform Heinsohn that Luis had already agreed to substitute for Irish.

Heinsohn, too, had an inner voice to suppress. 'You don't owe this girl any explanations,' it said. 'This is business.' He was vaguely annoyed with himself because it seemed important to him somehow that

148

Leonie think well of him. 'I'm not pulling out arbitrarily,' he insisted. 'I want to do what's best for the group. And I know it's a little tricky, coordinating the reading with the music. That can make or break the whole thing. I wouldn't want to louse it up for lack of practice.'

Leonie said thoughtfully, 'It just seems strange that you should have any business while on a cruise. I didn't think . . .' She caught herself hastily. 'Forgive me, Werner. It's absolutely none of my business. I didn't mean to pry.'

'That's all right,' he said, wondering at the small jab of conscience he felt, thinking how very much it *was* her business. That's what came of dealing with women, especially beautiful ones. It irritated him to have his professionalism threatened in any way. 'I just happen to be one of those unfortunates whose work knows no schedule or specific work days. I'm sometimes forced to combine business with pleasure.'

A thought struck her. 'Is that why you made the remark in Juneau about only being with us the rest of the week?'

Something moved behind his pale eyes and she thought the question had flustered him. Well, she ought to know enough not to ask someone like Werner Heinsohn questions. He was too private, too secretive. But he merely shrugged it off. 'I don't really remember what

149

I said. I've known for some time I had to attend to something in Homer.'

She might never have caught it if he had given her a direct answer, but his hesitation and momentary imbalance brought a sudden remembrance. She could recall clearly now that he had made a hasty amendment, as if he had misspoken. In Prince Rupert, after he had disappeared all morning (and that was odd!) her mother had asked, 'Will you be taking the tour in Juneau tomorrow?' And Heinsohn had replied, 'Oh, yes. I don't have a thing to do now but enjoy myself for the rest of the week.' Then had come the quick correction. 'I mean for two weeks.'

Then she remembered something else. The odd look that Irish had given him when he said it. Her father had caught it too. She could see it in his face. Why in the world had Werner bothered to lie? If he had something to detain him in Homer, why, that was nobody's business but his own. He was a very private person, that was plain, but why be so secretive about something as innocent as a business deal?

She shrugged it off, thinking: as they say, people are funny.

They had such an exhilarating time at the rehearsal that night that Leonie quite forgot Heinsohn's defection. She also failed to notice anything strange about Irish's insistence that the curtain behind them, hiding the band

150

instruments, be kept open. 'Not tonight.' He was firm when someone started to close them. 'We'll have it closed the night of the performance, of course.' Nor did she register the intensity of his gaze as his eyes swept the area thoroughly.

Luis Carrasco, with his bold Latin features and impressive mustache—his own—needed only the addition of a big hat, a fat cigar, and a colorful bandanna around his neck to make a marvelous Dan McGrew.

They had a hard time finding the necessary 'buckskin shirt that was glazed with dirt' for the judge, but finally unearthed a fringed leather jacket for him. He, too, sported an impressive mustache, not his own. With his rabbit-pelt beard pinned to an old fishing cap, only his nose and eyes showed, and he was quite unrecognizable as 'the stranger.'

Sanna, also adorned with a false mustache, her bright hair stuffed under a cap, looked like an adorable boy in overalls. Her lively rendition of the 'Maple Leaf Rag' initiated the action, and not for the first time, Leonie marveled at her mother's versatility at the piano. She could render the most difficult classical passages with equal ease.

The sounds of the music softened as Irish's magical voice began the opening lines of the famous poem: '"*A bunch of the boys were whooping it up in the Malamute Saloon. / The kid that handles the music box was hitting a*

151

rag-time tune. / Back of the bar, in a solo game, sat Dangerous Dan McGrew."'

Now the stirring tones of the 'William Tell Overture' identified Dangerous Dan as Luis pantomimed playing cards and made appropriately villainous faces.

'"*And watching his luck*," Irish went on, '"*was his light-of-love, the lady that's known as Lou.*"'

His rich voice brought new life and meaning to the familiar words as he spoke of the stranger, his life ruined by a faithless woman, appearing suddenly out of the freezing night to exact vengeance on the man who had stolen her from him. Although it was only a rehearsal of a ship's Talent Show, the performers felt their pulses quicken as the action built to a shattering climax, when the lights went out and a scream was heard, followed by the report of two guns.

The lights came back on, and Irish's thrilling voice heightened the drama as he read, '"*Pitched on his head, and pumped full of lead, was Dangerous Dan McGrew. / While the man from the creeks lay clutched to the breast of the lady that's known as Lou.*"'

Leonie could feel her heart pounding as she held her father close. How still he was! Was he that good an actor? Or could the dramatic action, the realistic gunshots possibly have caused his ailing heart to...

For a time-locked moment terror flared in

her like a white-hot flame, then the judge opened one eye, smiled sheepishly at her, and awkwardly got to his feet. The others looked sheepish, too, unwilling to admit they had been so emotionally caught up in the rehearsal of a skit.

Luis seemed absolutely exhilarated by the experience. 'But that was fantastic!' he said, as he rose to his feet. 'I don't remember when I last enjoyed something so much. I feel marvelous now. Nothing like a good murder or two to stir the blood!'

Maribel, uncaring that she could not understand the English words, felt her inward pain diminish somewhat as she watched his handsome face, flushed with excitement. She thought: if only he could be this happy for whatever time he has left to him!

CHAPTER FIFTEEN

ACTIVATE...
to set in motion.

The small ape-like man pulled the pickup camper, rented in Anchorage, into one of the few available spaces on the campground along Homer Spit and turned off the ignition with a sigh of relief. The two-hundred-plus-mile drive from Anchorage had been practically nonstop. It would be longer going back on the cycle, but was still the easiest money he'd earned in a long time.

The first fifty miles out of Anchorage, the highway had twisted and turned along the base of the Chugach Mountains, following the irregular shoreline of Turnagain Arm. But the spectacular scenery that so many paid so much to see had been lost to him. This was just another job. In his eyes a good one, paying much for doing little.

He'd had plenty of time to get ready since Heinsohn had called him, first from Prince Rupert, then from Juneau, to be sure he'd made all the necessary arrangements. Now all he lacked were the purchases on this end and the setup for Heinsohn to pick up the key to the vehicle. The job was even easier than he thought it would be, since they'd changed the original plans.

At first it was decided he would erect a makeshift dwelling on the beach like those used by the Spit Rats—mostly young people who had come to work in Homer but could not find or afford orthodox housing. Their solution had been to wrap some Visqueen plastic around a few poles, scrounge some driftwood for chairs and add campstove and lantern to make 'a home away from home.' You could hide there forever. But new regulations had gone into effect, putting restrictions on use of the Spit for camping

154

and instituting a nightly camping fee. That meant a fee collector prowling the area several times a day trying to find people home. So the plan had been changed to include the camper.

With hordes of campers and backpackers in town he knew it was unlikely anyone would have an interest in him. Even so, he disguised himself with wig, beard and glasses before buying groceries at Proctor's on Main Street. His simian features crinkled in amusement to think how different he looked from the man who had shopped in Proctor's at Anchorage.

Now all that remained was to leave the camper key and license number for Heinsohn. He put both in an envelope addressed to 'Sam Jones,' and, using his duplicate key, left them in the post office box Heinsohn had rented in that name on his preparatory trip to Homer. His money was already waiting in the box for him, as planned.

Back at the campsite, he wrestled out the big Honda motorcycle, using a makeshift ramp, and got ready to get under way. The rest was up to Heinsohn.

It never occurred to him to wonder what would require such elaborate preparations. He'd had much stranger orders to fill. He wasn't paid to think. He wasn't equipped for it anyway.

★   ★   ★

'You'll like Homer,' Dr. Barnes said at breakfast. He had taken the chair usually occupied by Irish, who was unaccountably missing. Where could he be? Leonie wondered, as she brought her attention back to the genial professor's remarks about Homer. 'You've probably heard that it's called the "Shangri-La of Alaska." The Homer Boat Harbor draws people from around the world. And no wonder. You have beautiful Kachemak Bay, ringed all around with snowy mountain peaks. You have fjords, glaciers, and dense spruce forests in the area. You have fantastic fishing. And the winter temperatures only occasionally fall below zero.'

Sanna said, 'It's odd the misconceptions people have about places they've never visited. I know better, but am still surprised that it's not cold up here in Alaska.'

'You are not alone.' Barnes laughed. 'My misconceptions were in reverse. I was telling Charlie Beardsley how foolish I felt when I accepted a friend's offer to go hunting with him in Texas. It was December, and we'd had a lot of snow here at home, and he'd been taunting me about the mild temperatures they were enjoying in "God's Country." Well, he lived in Houston, where winters are mild, but his ranch was in the Big Bend area. I should have remembered how diverse Terxas is in

156

terrain and climate, but I was foolish enough to think I wouldn't need any really warm clothing. By all the rules, I figured, Texas ought to be warm and dry, even in winter. That first night up in those high desert mountains it snowed, and I had to get up and put on everything I owned before I could get warm enough to get some rest!'

'But it does get dreadfully cold here in the winter, doesn't it?' Leonie asked.

'Well, that depends upon where you are. In the interior, certainly. But down on the Kenai Peninsula, where we'll be when we visit Homer, it's surprisingly mild because of the ocean current. However, if you live up on the bluff, as it's called, some 1600 feet higher than the town, you can expect six more weeks of winter and a colder one, because of the difference in altitude—right in the same area. What you really have to watch out for where cold is concerned is the wind-chill factor.'

Sanna said, 'I hear this mentioned on the weather reports all the time, but I'm not sure I really understand it, except to know that if there's wind you feel colder.'

'A lot of people don't understand the effect wind has in taking away body heat,' Barnes told her. 'It's just as important as the outside temperature. Air movement has a chilling effect because it carries away the thin layer of warm air that builds up near your body.'

John Warwick joined the conversation at

this point. 'Is that why so many hunters insist they have to carry a flask to protect themselves from the elements?'

His tone was amused, but Barnes' normally amiable expression did not reflect the humor. 'Not I,' he said, somewhat stiffly. 'That's a serious, and sometimes deadly mistake. Alcohol dilates the blood vessels and brings the blood closer to the surface. The result is excessive cooling. People are fooled because of the initial sensation of warmth. The sensible thing is to dress in layers and leave as little skin exposed as possible. The hands and face are particularly vulnerable. If you had an outside temperature of minus 20 degrees and a wind of only 20 miles per hour, the result would be an effective temperature of minus 68 degrees Fahrenheit. Your flesh would be frozen in about one minute.' He paused and flushed slightly with embarrassment. 'There I go sounding like a professor again. I was actually giving a lecture. Please forgive me. You must think me a pedantic killjoy.'

'Not at all,' Sanna assured him hastily, with her exquisite tact. 'These things are extremely important, and I'm sure many lives have been lost for lack of that knowledge. Although I don't think we're in any danger now,' she added, with her dry tone and wry smile. The general laughter that followed lightened the mood and provided a tacit changing of the subject. This gave John the opportunity to speak up again.

'Speaking of misconceptions,' he said, 'I was reading about a little old lady from L.A. who complained to the doctor about heart flutters while she was on a cruise ship. When he asked if her heart had ever bothered her before, she told him she had a problem only at a high altitude.

'The doctor assured her it had to be her digestion or something else because they'd been at sea level ever since the ship left Vancouver. To which she replied, "Oh, doctor, you don't understand. Why, you're so high up here you're halfway to the North Pole!"'

Leonie shook her head. 'We're laughing, but I wonder if we sometimes don't have just as confused ideas about other things. I, for one, always thought that totem poles were objects of worship for the Indians, but our lecturer said they were not.'

'They were never worshipped,' Dr. Barnes confirmed. 'And they are more than merely art. They are an important social record.'

Sanna put in, 'I love the way the lecturer described Indian art. He said, "Quality Indian art is like good cooking. It can be tasted but not explained." He was paraphrasing someone else, I forgot who, but I thought it was very apt.'

'Before we lose you,' the judge said, 'I want to ask a question. Did the great earthquake of

159

Good Friday, 1964, have an effect this far down?'

For a moment Barnes' face went very still. Then he answered, 'Indeed it did! Most of the Spit had to be rebuilt afterward. It dropped six feet—all of it. Although, of course, you can't tell that now. But you'll see some very dramatic after effects of the earthquake still visible when we get to Anchorage.'

It seemed to cost the professor some effort to discuss the subject, even at this late date, and Leonie wondered as they left the dining room if there might be a story there. But all her curiosity about Dr. Barnes' personal life fled as she spied Irish peering in to see if she was still there. She suddenly realized that she had glimpsed him several times before while they'd been eating, but had been so engrossed in the conversation she'd been only subliminally aware of it. The big Irishman was frowning slightly as he approached.

'What's the matter?' Leonie went to meet him, asking the question as naturally as if she were a long-time and close friend.

'Matter? Nothing's the matter. Why do you ask that?'

'You look as if you're concerned about something. I just can't imagine you being nervous, but you seem all tensed up.' Then she caught herself. 'Forgive me if that sounds nosy.'

160

He did not reply to this, but relaxed with a conscious effort after one sharp look at her. Why did the girl have to be so perceptive? Her sensitivity to other people's vibrations was more evident to him with each encounter. If she'd only known the tension building within him—and its cause—she would not possibly be able to stand there so lazily relaxed.

He forced a big grin, but said nothing before he was saved by the arrival of the senior Warwicks who had stopped to chat on their way out. The conversation was very general after that, before they left to prepare themselves for their full day in Homer.

As they gathered in Purser's Square for a shore excursion soon afterward, securing their identification cards, she saw Werner Heinsohn striding purposefully toward her. Almost in the same moment she spied Irish, who was craning in all directions trying to locate her. A strange expression crossed his face when he realized Heinsohn would reach her first. There was just one word for it: consternation.

Leonie misinterpreted this look and a spirit of perversity seized her. It was time, she decided, to play a little hard to get. She was so intent on planning her strategy that she failed to notice her father's preoccupation. Sanna had noticed but didn't think it important enough to ask about the cause.

John would not have confided in his wife even if she had asked what was on his mind. He had just received the disturbing message from his district attorney's office that Alfredo Petrosino had escaped and was, presumably, arranging to carry out his threat of vengeance. He smiled a tight little smile to himself. The second half of the message was supposed to put his mind at rest: there was an undercover FBI man on board, guarding him.

So! His instincts had been right! Although he had taken quite a liking to young Callahan, he was sure now who he was, and knew he must not allow Leonie to see him again after the trip was over. Heinsohn, of course, was the FBI agent sent to protect him. That explained his hard-eyed wariness, his constant air of being on the alert. There was some consolation in the thought of having such a formidable guard dog.

He caught Sanna looking at him anxiously and realized he must be presenting a frowning, grim-faced visage. No need to worry the women. They were having such a good time here. He forced a smile and took his wife's arm as the announcement came for their departure. 'Just day-dreaming,' he soothed her. 'Here we go for another great adventure. Anchors aweigh!'

CHAPTER SIXTEEN

PREVARICATE...
to stray from or evade the truth.

The sea was so choppy that Leonie wondered briefly if her introduction to Homer was to be a frosty dip. With water temperatures of forty-six to fifty-one degrees in the summertime, only the unwary or foolish-of-heart braved the chilly waters to swim. The little tender heaved and bounced, but Leonie finally managed to get ashore, with the help of some fancy footwork and several very willing strong arms. Among these were Werner Heinsohn's. She looked up at him, laughing.

'You always seem to be setting me back on my feet. Of course,' she observed, 'the first time it was also you who knocked me off them.'

'That's the wrong word,' Heinsohn informed her, smiling gravely down from his great height. 'You're supposed to say I *swept* you off your feet.

'Okay, have it your way.' Leonie began to laugh again, then sobered quickly as a clear memory, submerged until this moment, surfaced: their first encounter.

'Werner, there's something I've been
163

meaning to ask you,' she began. 'That first time we met, you were holding...' She was interrupted by his huge hand on her arm and a look of great concentration on his usually impassive face.

She tried to interpret that look. It was intense, earnest, pleading, all at once. Perhaps he had guessed what she was about to ask, and would be embarrassed by an explanation of why he was carrying her picture around. Perhaps he had even engineered that encounter in order to meet her. It seemed somewhat out of character for him, more like Irish's speed. And she might just be flattering herself, but what other explanation was there? Well, there was no need to embarrass him. So sure was she that he was following her own line of thought that she was completely unprepared when he demonstrated otherwise as he drew her aside.

'Leonie, please,' he began, 'before the others descend on us I want to ask a favor.'

'What sort of favor?' She could not hide her surprise.

He hesitated a moment, his expression unreadable now, and Leonie wondered if he could possibly be displaying shyness. He was certainly not as bold and outgoing as Irish, in fact seemed reticent only by comparison, but she could not imagine him as shy. She'd ask some other time about that clipping. Right now he seemed to have a problem.

'What is it, Werner?' she encouraged him.

'Well,' he said slowly, 'you know Irish had you all to himself in Prince Rupert. Give me a break. Let me rent a car and show you around Homer. Okay?'

Was that all he wanted? Why make a big production of it? He was an absolutely unfathomable man. She did enjoy being with him, but he could be so *intense*. Well, if he wanted nothing more than the pleasure of her company on a beautiful day, that was just the opportunity she needed to see that a certain Irishman didn't get ideas. That boy was much too sure of himself!'

'Of course!' she said enthusiastically. 'I'll just tell my folks. They won't mind my running off on my own. They'd expect me to. In fact...' She stopped, flirting a little with a sideways amber-tinted green gaze. 'In fact, they'd tell me how fortunate I was to have a handsome man squire me around.' Even as she played up to him she wondered at herself. This was just not in character. Was she that fearful of emotional involvement with Irish? She refused to consider that question just now.

So intent was Leonie on putting Irish out of her mind and concentrating on Heinsohn, that she did not notice her father's look of almost shocked surprise when she came to announce her intentions. If she had, she would have attributed it to her obvious

165

preference for Irish's company. As Sanna was now doing.

But John was more than surprised. He was stunned. What sort of bodyguard went off and left his charge all day? Oh, well, he reasoned to himself, we'll be in a crowd of people, all of whom we know by sight. Heinsohn knows that, too. Why shouldn't the boy have a little fun? I'm acting like a timid old lady!

As they left the boat ramp, Heinsohn waved a sweeping hand at the long finger of land jutting out into the water. 'There you are. Homer Spit. Over five miles long and the second longest spit in the world. Ringed by beautiful Kachemak Bay and home of the famous Salty Dawg Saloon and other wonders of the world.'

'What have we here?' Leonie teased. 'Sanna the Second? Are you another one who finds out everything about a place before you visit?'

'Precisely, madam. While you were dancing the night away with that big lout of an Irishman, I was down in the theatre absorbing the lecture on Homer. Very instructive. Just the thing to impress a young lady you hoped to monopolize for a whole day.' His smile seemed entirely free of reserve now.

'I'm ready to go,' Leonie declared.

'That's great! There's some absolutely

incredible scenery. We can drive up on the bluff and get a fantastic view of the town, the Spit, the bay, and the mountains all around. And there are berries and wildflowers. Whole fields of fireweed. Wait until you see the hills blanketed with them!'

Leonie looked at him curiously, marveling at his uncharacteristic eloquence. 'You sound like a travel folder,' she remarked. 'Did you learn all this from the lecture, or have you been here before?'

'Not really,' Heinsohn replied, rather shortly, and his face seemed to close. He could hardly mention that just before the cruise began he had made a quick trip to Homer to reconnoiter possibilities for her kidnapping, hopping a flight from Anchorage to join the others aboard ship in Vancouver just before they sailed.

Leonie thought: what a strange reply. 'Not really.' What kind of answer was that? You either had been somewhere or you hadn't. Yet it sounded familiar. Then remembrance flickered. Of course! She'd heard the same answer before, when Sanna asked Irish if he'd ever been to Europe and he had given the same peculiar reply. How very odd.

She realized she'd missed something Heinsohn was saying and apologized, mentally shrugging the small mystery away. It couldn't be very important. 'I'm sorry, Werner. I was daydreaming a little. What did you say?'

'I said I thought it would be fun to have lunch at Land's End after we take our tour. There's a marvelous view of Kachemak Bay.'

'What's Land's End?'

'It's a resort hotel, right on the tip of the Spit. It sports a dining room, cocktail lounge complete with dance floor, and a gift shop. You can see,' he added hastily as her look sharpened once more, 'that I've been boning up on places to go and things to see in Homer.'

The glib explanation erased the last of Leonie's fleeting curiosity for the moment, and she felt nothing but anticipation at the thought of a pleasant day in Heinsohn's company. He was a little reserved, but good fun, and always gentlemanly in his behavior. She smiled at herself, at the old-fashioned tone of her assessment, then frowned as the thought came, unbidden: I'd really rather be with that brash Irishman. Well, it won't hurt for him to have a little competition. Unconsciously she tossed her head in a small gesture of defiance before she turned her attention fully to Werner Heinsohn.

'Where do we go first?' she asked.

'Well, if we're going to drive anywhere we'll need a car,' he pointed out reasonably. 'I'll call for one.'

They had reached the road by now, and he turned toward a wooden building on their

168

right. 'This is the Harbormaster's office. There's a pay phone here. Do we want to get the car now and do our sightseeing, or would you prefer to do some walking and visit the town, then get a car and take the scenic tour? It's up to you.'

'How far is it?' Leonie asked. 'A walk would be fun, if it isn't too far.'

'It's about six miles to town, but only what they call "a good walk" to Land's End.'

Leonie was dubious. 'I'm not sure I could manage six miles,' she said. 'Besides, I want to see everything there is to see, and we really don't have all that much time. We have to be back on board rather early: 4:00 P.M., I think they said. Why don't we call for the car, tour the town, then take your scenic drive? That won't give us much exercise, but it would give us more time for everything before we come back to Land's End for lunch. Do you suppose we can find a good home for these box lunches the ship provided?'

'No doubt about it!' he said emphatically.

Leonie looked surprised at his tone of absolute conviction. 'How do you know? You sounded as though you had someone already picked out for recipients. Seagulls?'

'No.' Heinsohn laughed. 'Spit Rats.'

'Spit *what?*'

'Spit Rats.' He waved his outsized hand toward the beach. 'Come on. You can see for yourself and I'll tell you something about them as we walk.'

They linked arms and moved closer to the beach. The area was cluttered with every kind of camping arrangement. Leonie looked with something like horror at the incredible collection, ranging from RVs to inadequate-looking tents to poles-and-plastic concoctions comprising the roughest of the lean-tos. 'You mean people *live* in those things?' she said, pointing.

'They do when housing is short and they can't afford anything else.' His tone was curt, almost accusing. 'Not everyone has oil interests in Alaska, you know.' Then he caught himself, aghast. 'I'm sorry, Leonie. I don't know what got into me, talking like that.' His tight little smile was back. 'It's perfectly all right to own oil wells in Alaska.'

Leonie stared at him, astonished. Could he possibly know of her father's oil interests here? Well, she answered herself promptly, he couldn't. It was just a generalized remark she had taken personally. He was certainly not one of the have-nots, obviously well-educated, polished enough, and beautifully dressed. And all that took money.

She bit off the retort that had been on the tip of her tongue, determined to let nothing mar the beauty and excitement of a lovely day in an enchanting setting. 'Tell me about Homer.'

'It's a fascinating place,' Heinsohn went on with a depth of feeling she had rarely heard in him. 'They call it the "Shangri-La of Alaska", you know. I'd love to retire here someday.

Retire from what? Leonie wondered. He never did say what his business was. She started to voice the question, but he spoke first.

'Besides the spectacular scenery, you have all sorts of birds and wild game, to say nothing of shrimp, halibut, shellfish, king and dungeness crab, and five kinds of salmon! Scientific studies show Kachemak to be the richest life-producing bay in the world.'

'I've heard there is quite an artists' colony here,' Leonie said.

'Yes, there is. And many individual studios. One famous lady paints with octopus ink! I'll tell you about it over lunch, if you're interested.'

He smiled down at her, amused by her childlike eagerness, but this time she did not catch the tinge of sadness in his smile. He had never known anyone like this girl, and it was becoming increasingly difficult to see the actions he had planned for that afternoon in a completely impersonal light.

It was impossible to keep from comparing her with Donna. About the only thing they had in common was music. Even then, a concert pianist and a nightclub singer were

171

hardly in the same category. Of course, they were both beautiful women, but there was a vast difference even there. Donna had the beauty of a full-blown rose. She would probably not be attractive in her later years. But Leonie had the fine bone structure and classical features that wore well. She would look much like her mother when she reached that age. Still a beauty, provided she stayed out of the sun and did not eat too much!

'Now you're the one who's daydreaming,' Leonie accused him.

'Sorry.' He came back to the present abruptly. 'I guess my mind did wander.'

'It must be the magic of this place.' She gave them both alibis. 'It's easy to just wander off into time and space.'

'You can't get too much out of touch with reality,' he said with a laugh, 'or you'll find yourself under water.'

'What do you mean?'

'If you live in Homer, you go in and out with the tide.'

'What in the world does that mean?' She wasn't too sure he was serious, but he was usually a little too sober-minded to do much teasing.

'You remember when we were checking the big map posted on the ship?' he asked. 'I showed you how Cook Inlet splits into two arms. Well, on paper the bottleneck appears mild, but the funneling effect on the water is terrific. The tides here go from fourteen to over thirty feet in just six hours.'

'They keep an eye on that water then!' she agreed.

'You can bet on it. People around here carry more tide books than Bibles—two or three in the house, one in each car, one in the boat, and one in the pocket. You just don't plan anything without consulting your tide book. You can imagine the problem it is with strangers to the area. You park a car or camper innocently and come back in a few hours to find it inundated. Even ebb tides are important. When the tide is out, the inhabitants rush to go clamming. The clams squirting all over the beach make the place look like one giant lawn sprinkler!'

'You talk like an old-timer,' she remarked, her curiosity surfacing again. 'And you've never been here before?'

'I have friends here,' he evaded, 'but no, I've never lived here.' He wasn't too happy with the turn of the conversation and looked around for a distraction. He found it in the sight of some young men throwing Frisbees, an ecstatic big black dog very much in the act.

'Look at that Labrador!' he exclaimed. 'What a jump! Isn't it fantastic how they time their leaps to get those things? They're hard enough for people to catch.' Then he added, unexpectedly, 'I miss my dog.'

'What kind do you have?' she asked.

'An Irish setter. Sean. And he's a beauty.'

Leonie watched his face light up and soften as he spoke. What a contradiction he was! Sometimes he seemed like a tightly-wound mainspring, ready to snap at any moment. There was a hard brilliance to him, a cold glitter to his deep-set eyes that hinted at the pressures and abrasions that make and polish a rough diamond. His beauty, too, seemed hard and cold, yet he had a streak of sentimentality that allowed such feeling for an animal.

She tried to imagine him rolling on the ground or gamboling with a dog, but could not. She couldn't conceive of his letting go like that. Something had happened in his childhood, she decided, to make him believe he dare not show his true feelings. Yet she had the odd feeling that there was an urgency in him, some driving force that was constantly goading him on. To what, she couldn't imagine.

A thought surfaced. Could it be rejection he feared? She had a sudden vivid memory of playing for a civic group that was entertaining some orphans at Christmastime. One boy stood out among the rest. A handsome boy, physically much larger and stronger-looking than the rest, he got a lot of attention but kept himself withdrawn from the activities, his face a careful mask of indifference. Yet he

174

could not restrain his ecstatic reaction to a hauntingly beautiful arrangement she had played of Christmas carols.

'Poor child,' the director had whispered later in answer to Leonie's expression of interest. 'He's been so rejected he's afraid to show love for anything. We're gradually getting him to show some involvement and even a little affection since we included him in a special little band. He loves music so.'

Leonie considered now what there might be in Heinsohn's past life to cause the erection of those invisible but terribly effective barriers that seemed to separate him from others. Maybe she should make more effort to draw him out, soften his lone wolf image. She knew now she could never have any romantic feeling for him, but she sensed some deep need in him, as she had in the orphan boy, and longed to reach him.

They called for the car, and explored the beauties of the bluff behind the city, then toured the Pratt Museum and the rustically charming home of 'Alaska Wild Berry Products.' A stop at the 'Taster's Stand' proved the claims made for the succulent hand-picked wild berries which were transformed into delicious jams, jellies, sauces and syrups.

Going back down the Spit, he introduced her to the Salty Dawg Saloon, looking like the lighthouse it once was. 'It's very famous,' he told her, 'although it's not as old as the Red Dog in Juneau.'

Once more she shook her head sadly at the sight of the Spit Rats, but made no further comment. He saw the look and laughed shortly. '"Poles-and-plastic," you said. That's about right. They say Visqueen plastic holds Alaska together. And, like everyplace else, you see the contrasts. You look at this, and then remember that land on Ocean Drive, the road between Beluga Lake and the Spit, is selling for handreds of dollars a square foot.' He stopped, and with a swing of mood said, 'Come on! Let's feed you. I promise you a superb lunch and an absolutely unbeatable view.'

At Land's End, as she drank in the glory of the mountains across the bay, Leonie was again aware of a subtle change in Werner Heinsohn, and she felt a growing uneasiness. Her sensitive perceptions, completely apart from her reasoning, signaled something in the man that was building toward enormous tension. It's almost, she told herself, as if that taut mainspring were attached to a bomb which was due to explode at a predetermined time.

How absurd you are! she scolded herself. But the inexplicable feeling of concern remained while the reason for it eluded her.

CHAPTER SEVENTEEN

PERPETRATE...
to commit, to accomplish.

Leonie never found out about the lady and the octopus ink. Her last memory of Homer was a sip of coffee and a last lingering look at the beauty of the mountains encircling Kachemak Bay. Her next sensation was of the unmistakable movement of a vehicle on a paved road.

Apparently he'd been watching her closely, even while driving, for he spoke even before she opened her eyes.

'How do you feel?'

Her eyes opened slowly then to meet Heinsohn's brief, impersonal gaze before he returned his attention back to the road. She still could not focus properly, but her mind was getting clearer every moment.

She raised herself slightly from the bunk where she lay, to glare at his clean-cut profile through the opened glass divider of the pickup-camper.

Her first word was a croak, and she had to swallow to moisten her cotton-dry mouth before she could speak. 'You put something in my coffee at lunch, didn't you?' she accused him.

'I'm sorry, Leonie, but that's the only way I could have gotten you here.'

'But why, Werner, *why?*' she wailed. 'What are we doing in this thing instead of being on the ship? Where are you taking me?' Her hands were trembling as she pushed the heavy auburn hair out of her eyes.

'It's a long story, Leonie, and you have a right to know.' He interrupted himself to speak again. 'How do you feel?'

'I'm okay,' she said in a carefully flat tone. 'Just a little headache.' She was determined to hide her fright and bewilderment as best she could, but she could not control the shaking of those traitorous hands. She clenched them tightly in her lap.

'I'm sorry about this,' he said. 'Really I am. But you'll understand soon why this was the only way to do it.'

'Do what?' she exploded, then winced as pain jabbed her temples. She lowered her voice then, forcing control. 'Do you realize I don't have the faintest idea of what you're talking about?'

'I know, I know,' he said soothingly. 'It must all seem very strange to you, but believe me, there is a reason for all this. Now look, if you really feel okay we'll stop as soon as we can, get you a cup of coffee, and I'll try to explain. But first, I must have your word you won't try to get away or get help. There's really no need to, and you'll understand this

178

if you give me a chance to tell you what's going on. What do you say?'

Her strength was returning rapidly and with it came a searing anger. 'I'll promise you nothing!' she cried. 'What right do you have to snatch me away in the middle of a cruise like this? My parents must be frantic.' She stopped short, enlightenment blazing in her. Suddenly, it all fell into place. A man carrying her picture around, cultivating her friendship, dancing attendance on her, all leading up to this moment. 'So that's it.' The contempt in her voice was scathing. 'A kidnaping because my father is a wealthy man. That's what this is all about.' The last was a statement, not a question.

He interrupted her brusquely. 'Leonie, please. We'll get nowhere this way. It's *not* what you think, not really. And you are in no danger from me whatsoever. Try to believe that.' He spoke very slowly and deliberately then, as if to force her understanding. 'This is a business proposition, and while I'm sorry to upset you and your folks like this, it's the only way I can...'

She cut him off, glaring. '*Business* proposition!' She was even whiter now, anger added to her shock. 'I don't believe this! How despicable. Pretending to make friends with me...'

'Leonie, please, calm down,' he pleaded. 'You'll only make yourself sick.' She was so

179

upset she was trembling all over now, and when she raised a shaking hand again to her forehead in a touching gesture of complete despair, he could feel his cool professionalism slipping. Where was his famed objectivity? At the moment he wanted nothing so much as to take her in his arms and soothe her fear away and somehow make her understand he was not a monster.

He decided to tip his hand, marveling at the taming of a man known throughout organized crime circles as The Hun. 'Leonie, you mustn't think too badly of me. It's not the way it appears. This doesn't concern you so much as your father and his safety. His *life* actually,' he amended bluntly. 'If you'll only believe I am honestly trying to save your father's life, I'll try to explain.'

He had her attention now. 'Werner, is that true?' She had crept up closer to the dividing window and leaned through now, trying to search his face as he watched the road. 'Why would you have to kidnap me to save him? It does take some believing, you'll have to admit.'

His pale eyes were cold, and a muscle twitched angrily in his cheek as he tried to check his impatience. 'Why can't you just trust me? I had to be devious, yes, but I am not a common kidnaper. And you'd better believe something else. At this point in time I am the *only* person who can save the judge.

He's a marked man, and his killer is on that ship! Now, are you going to listen to me or not?'

Her color had gone from white to gray, and he was suddenly fearful that she would slip back into unconsciousness. 'Lie back down,' he ordered gruffly, but the hostility was gone from his voice. 'When you're feeling better we'll stop and I'll put you fully in the picture. Okay?'

'All right,' she answered, woodenly, slipping bonelessly back down onto the bunk, closing her eyes, her mind exploding with turbulent thoughts. This couldn't really be happening, could it? She felt oddly detached from her body, separated from reality.

'Leonie?' His voice penetrated the suffocating fog that seemed to envelop her.

'I'm awake.' She sat up slowly, like a tired old lady. 'Where are we?'

'We're near Cooper Landing. We'll stop at Hamilton's Place. It's very nice, and we can get food, drink and service for the pickup.'

She noted again his obvious familiarity with the area they were in. How carefully it had all been planned! But to her own surprise she found herself suddenly accepting, resigned. Some kind of survival mechanism, she supposed. Only now did she give any heed to her surroundings.

The Kenai River flowed directly alongside the Sterling Highway on which they rode, with lush strands of spruce marching boldly up toward the suddenly soaring hills. Nothing bespoke her condition better than the indifference she showed to the beautiful scene.

Once in the restaurant, she sat listlessly, toying with her coffee cup, waiting for him to make the first move.

'Want something to eat?'

'No, I'm not hungry.' She suddenly remembered their last meal together. Her face must have reflected her thoughts for he said softly, 'Leonie, look at me. Are you afraid of me?'

She spoke carefully now, unsure of this man who had so abruptly became a stranger. 'Afraid of you? Yes, I guess I am.' Her voice strengthened as anger reappeared. 'How would you feel if someone you knew'—her chin lifted defiantly—'and liked, suddenly turned from a new friend into a threat?' Her eyes challenged him as she spoke, bravado now peeking through the fear. 'And yet you want me to believe that kidnaping me will somehow save my father's life.'

He looked around. There was no one nearby who could possibly be interested in them, but he lowered his voice as he leaned across the table to take her cold, unresisting hand.

'Leonie,' he insisted, 'you've got to trust me. I can't stand for you to be afraid of me.'

'Honestly, Werner,' she burst out, coming to life and snatching back her hand. 'You're too much. Do you think I would just be intrigued and delighted to interrupt a marvelous cruise and scare my parents to death just to go prancing off with you?' She had recovered enough to sound indignant. 'That I'd jump at the chance to help you extort money from my own father?'

'Leonie,' his tone was exasperated, 'you just don't understand. *I* don't want or need your father's money. And if someone else had this assignment, your lack of cooperation would be signing his death warrant.'

Even with her mind in turmoil she picked up on the crucial word. '*Assignment?* You mean you're doing this for someone else?' Her mind raced ahead. If he were a law enforcement officer of some kind, wouldn't he have shown his credentials at once and put her mind at rest? Would a legitimate lawman have taken her like this without first explaining the situation and getting her cooperation? No.

'I don't believe you,' she said flatly. 'If you're on assignment, why didn't you identify yourself instead of scaring me to death like that? You could just have *told* me, for heaven's sake! You didn't need to *drug* me. Kidnap me!' Her voice, which had become shrill with italics, dropped abruptly, like a plummeting elevator. 'How do you expect me to believe you when we're here instead of back on the ship looking after my father?' Her voice rose again, each word a note higher on the scale. She was dangerously close to hysteria.

Heads were beginning to turn, and he rose abruptly. 'Let's get out of here. We need to talk in private. I can see that nothing but the whole truth will convince you.'

He led her, numb and unresisting, to the door.

CHAPTER EIGHTEEN

ILLUMINATE...
to clarify, to make understandable.

She sat beside him in the camper, determined to subdue her fear and keep her mind open to anything that might shed more light on the whole bizarre situation.

'You remember the man who threatened your father on his last case?' he began without preamble.

'Petrosino?' She was startled. 'But he's dead!'

Heinsohn shook his massive head vehemently, sending the fine blond hair in all directions. 'Everyone's supposed to think so, but he's not. He's very much alive. He's not directly in the picture now; he's retired.' The sarcastic emphasis on the last word reflected his opinion of the obscenity of Petrosino's career as head of a crime syndicate, and brought a speculative look from Leonie. 'He thinks I'm working for him,' Heinsohn continued. 'I have in the past, so that I could worm my way into his confidence, and now I finally have the chance I've waited so long for—to work against him.' He stopped; his face took on a faraway look that told her he was speaking of something that had gripped his heart and occupied his mind for a long time. She sat quietly, without moving, until he came out of his brief reverie.

'I can't reach him directly now,' he went on, his voice so expressionless and full of menace it sent chills up the girl's back, 'but I can destroy his empire by getting to his lieutenant—the man who's taking over from him. Without him, the whole organization will fall apart. They'll be wiped out by rival mobs in no time. The opposition has already made an attempt on the successor's life. Everybody thought they'd succeeded, but apparently, by some miracle, they hadn't hit him as hard as they thought they had. Now I'm in the perfect position to eliminate him because I have no connection with any of the rivals. He won't suspect me at all.'

'Eliminate?' She choked on the word. 'You mean you're going to *kill* him?'

He raised a pleading hand as she shrank from him, eyes wide with horror. 'Wait a minute! Listen to me! In the first place, I'll be doing you a favor. If he's not eliminated, your father will be. Which would you prefer?'

'But you just can't kill people like that!' She was practically spluttering in her distress. 'Why can't you just tip the authorities off and have them apprehend him on the ship?'

'Tip them off to what?' he demanded. 'Just how would I go about proving he was planning to murder the judge on Petrosino's orders? He'd make a laughing stock of me, especially now that Petrosino is presumed dead. With no evidence, nothing but my unsupported accusations? Don't be a fool!' His voice was harsh with anger. 'Besides, this is a personal thing with me. We'll just keep it simple.'

She was so appalled at his reasoning she forgot to be afraid. 'But you can't justify killing people like that, even criminals, just because they're bad,' she said hotly. 'Unless you're defending yourself.'

'How about defending someone you loved very much? Would you break a few rules then? That's the trouble with you so-called "good" people. You're out of touch with reality! There was even some churchman, a bishop, I think, who once said, "One murder makes a villain, millions a hero."'

'Well, if you're going to quote,' she

186

declared, 'there's an old proverb that says, "Conscience is the voice of God speaking to the soul." Don't you have a conscience?'

He ignored that completely. 'I know the Bible says not to kill,' he went on, 'but it also says something about not shedding *innocent* blood, doesn't it? And "those who live by the sword shall die by the sword."'

Not for the first time, Leonie marveled at the way people were prone to use the Scriptures to justify their own point of view. She was about to comment when he spoke again. His tone had changed abruptly. 'Let me tell you a story,' he said. 'Maybe it will help you to see things my way.'

'Okay,' she said tonelessly, knowing she was not going to reach him by reasoning or advancing concepts of Christian belief. She sank back with a feeling of complete detachment from the everyday world, senses dulled by the incredibility of it all.

He began to talk about his father, a much-decorated police officer. A man who, to an impressionable youngster, could do no wrong. A hero, a giant-killer whose image grew larger and brighter until it was impossibly idealized. Then his father was killed, gunned down by the man who controlled much of the underworld's activities: Alfredo Petrosino.

As he spoke his voice took on an oddly flat tone, the self-protecting lack of expression one would use in retelling an atrocity. 'My father was killed by the same man who wants to see your father dead,' he said. 'And for the same reason. They couldn't be bribed, couldn't be bought. Wolfgang Heinsohn, captain of police, lived for just one thing: to rid the world of such people. And he taught me that for this country of ours to survive and be like it used to be, we have to wipe out all the vermin—the pimps, the junkies with their scrambled brains, the pushers who sell them the stuff, the racketeers who break people's legs and destroy their businesses when they won't pay "protection" money.' He stopped for breath, then shrugged and exhaled slowly, realizing he was getting carried away. His voice resumed its normal expression as he went on. 'Of course, all the scum screamed "police brutality!" but he got results no one else achieved.

'I guess it sounds crazy to you, but I'm doing all of us a favor. You know, when my mother remarried, soon after my father's death...' He stopped, and it was obvious the emotion that twisted his face was also twisting his guts. 'Well, anyway,' he resumed, his expression now carefully guarded, 'I ran off, joined the Marines, and went to Nam. I was just a kid, but I learned to kill people—efficiently. They made me understand that if I didn't, this country would be overrun by the Commies and their ilk, people who didn't think other people had any rights at all. Well, my father gave his life in a different kind of war, to keep a different kind of enemy from taking us over. And now that I'm grown, I haven't changed my opinion on that point at all.

'The career criminal is a blight, a cancer that will completely destroy our way of life if we don't stop him—any way we can. The courts are too soft, the system too overloaded and too antiquated. To say nothing of corrupt. Something has to be done.'

She interrupted his impassioned flow of words to ask softly, 'Your mother—is she still alive?'

He stared at her. 'I don't even know. The last time I saw her she was getting ready to leave on her honeymoon with her new husband.' His mouth twisted again in spite of himself. 'He wasn't even a policeman; he was an accountant.' He made no effort to hide his contempt.

Leonie could imagine his adolescent anguish, his youthful assessment of his mother as a traitor, faithless to the memory of an incomparable man. And she could visualize him swearing to take up the sword, so to speak, from the fallen hero, eager to wreak vengeance in the grand tradition on the evildoers who had taken his father's life.

But he was no longer a child. Had his character development been arrested then, traumatized by the brutal events of his father's murder? Or had he simply never gotten above the level of his emotions, viewing events only through them, excluding reason? She had to know. There was too much good in this man to be wasted. At the least she must make some effort to get him to realize that no matter what his background or the forces that shaped him, he must act as a mature adult, taking responsibility for his actions. And to realize that without the structure of law and order, imperfect as it was, anarchy would prevail and the world would be even more of a jungle than it now appeared to be.

'Tell me,' she said, her voice still very soft, coaxing, as if she were approaching a dangerous animal. 'What were your mother's feelings about all this—that is, about your father—what he did and how he did it? Have you thought about all this from her point of view?' She saw immediately from his expression that she had touched a nerve, and sat very still, leaving him to his thoughts.

Her question startled him. For the first time he caught a glimpse of meaning, of explanation, behind his mother's vague and indirect remarks. He hadn't given them a thought since his childhood. What was it she had said: 'I'm not going to say anything against your father, Werner. He's dead and can't defend himself. But later, when you're fully grown, you'll understand and know I'm doing the right thing in trying to make a better life for myself.'

'A better life?' She had made no effort to elaborate, and although he had been fully grown for some time now, he had never bothered to try to understand. In fact, he had determined so fiercely to put her apparent defection out of his mind that he had scarcely thought of her at all in the ensuing years.

When he was a child she had been a quiet, hardworking shadow, ministering to his needs kindly and uncomplainingly, but with a lack of warmth that he did not miss because of the burning brightness of the father image that filled his mind with tales of danger and dragon-slaying in which only one person starred: Captain Wolfgang Heinsohn. 'Wolf' they had called him, and wolf he had been. Tough, ruthless and resourceful, fearing nothing. Never had it occurred to the young Werner that the fascinating stories might have been exaggerated. There was no doubt of his father's status as a hero. That much was documented. How could his courage ever be questioned? But other questions began to form in the back of his mind now that he had been led into a review of the situation from a more adult perspective. There had been no quiet retelling of incidents, no understatements, no modesty. Unnoted by Werner the young boy, Werner the man considered for the first time in his life the possibility of bombast and brutality, sadism and self-importance masking insecurity.

He felt a blinding flash of insight. Somehow he knew in his heart now, with an appalling certainty, that his youthful idol was far from the man he had worshipped. In a burst of revelation, from buried bits of information quietly computed in his brain over the years, he now realized that his mother had not been unnaturally quiet, but simply subdued by brutality and intimidation.

The silence lengthened until Leonie finally broke it. Her voice held the careful tone one would use in waking a sleepwalker. 'Werner?' It was almost a whisper. He looked at her blankly, as if he had indeed been sleepwalking. 'Werner,' she continued softly, 'time passes, and we pass with it. And the saddest words in the world are "if only." There's a West African proverb that says: "When someone helps you cut your teeth, you must help them cut their meat." I hope you'll contact your mother.'

He gave her a long appraising look, almost too long for safety at the speed they were traveling. 'Leonie,' he said, 'you're quite a girl.'

Up until now he had had little opportunity to see past her outward appearance, but he realized that his assessment of her had

192

changed drastically in the last few hours. At first he had put her down as a beautiful featherweight, a glamor girl who didn't have enough character to make a marriage stick. Now he regretted that quick judgment and felt shame in misjudging her so badly. It suddenly occurred to him that while his professional judgments—even the split-second ones—were invariably correct, more often than not his personal judgments were way off. The thought teased his mind that perhaps where his father was concerned, too, he had seen only what he wanted to see. And hadn't seen his mother's side at all.

Was he getting sentimental as he grew older? Well, sentiment had no place in this serious business. He might find his mother one day, let her know he wanted to reestablish their relationship on a more adult level. But none of that changed the problem of Petrosino. He and his ilk must somehow be removed from the lives of decent people. Leonie had to be made to understand that.

He repeated, 'Yes, quite a girl. You're not only beautiful, but you've got guts as well. It's important to me that you don't have the wrong impression of what kind of person I am.'

'Do you know what I think you are?' she asked. There were sorry and pity in her look now. 'I think you are terribly misguided. I have the feeling you were reared by a mother

193

who worked hard to instill concepts of justice in you, and a father who got them all mixed up.'

He bristled immediately. 'You make me sound like some kind of monster. My ridding the world of vermin may make me an exterminator, but I'm not a murderer! If you believe all that pap the preachers put out, about loving your enemies and returning good for evil, you must be out of touch with reality for sure!'

She refused to be baited. Aware it would be useless to preach to him in his present frame of mind, she nonetheless felt compelled to advance the most important point for his consideration. 'Most people completely misinterpret that bit of scripture, because we only have the one word, "love," in our language to express so many different emotions. Other languages are much richer. Reduced to its simplest terms it means that as a Christian you don't even have to *like* a person to be willing to do what's right for him, no matter how he's treated you.'

She spoke softly, but his face grew cold with anger at this threat to his holy crusade. 'You've been listening to too many of those sanctimonious preachers!' he rasped. 'The more self-righteous they are, the more suspicious I get that they're not all they should be.'

Leonie could feel every nerve bristling at
194

his unfair generalization, especially as she thought of their own hardworking, self-sacrificing minister. 'Of course there are hypocrites in the church,' she said hotly. 'There are hypocrites everywhere. But the fault lies with the imperfection of human beings, not the system. Yet most of the Christians I know try very hard to follow the teachings of their religion, knowing all too well how easy it is to be tempted into doing wrong.'

He brushed away her attitudes on morality with the impatient gesture of one removing an annoying insect. 'I don't want to hear any more of that nonsense,' he said disdainfully. 'I've got more important things to think about.'

She capitulated, knowing that further argument would only increase his resistance and his anger. There was something she had to know. If she hadn't already made him too angry to speak further. She put a hesitant hand on his hugely muscled arm. 'Werner, who is the man who is a threat to my father? Don't I have the right to know?'

'Maybe,' he said stiffly, 'but I can't tell you that. If you knew, you'd show it, and that would ruin everything. You see, I know the plan for killing your father—when, where and how the hit man plans to do it. If all of you acted suspicious of him, or changed your attitudes toward him in any way...' He caught her startled look and nodded. 'Yes, it's someone you know. And, as I say, if you act at all different he'll know the information could have come only from me. Then he'll simply change his plans and not tell me, and probably kill me too. Then where would your father be?'

'But surely no one could expect to kill someone on board ship like that and get away with it!' she burst out.

He looked at her pityingly. 'You'd be surprised,' he said ominously. 'People in your world just don't understand how easy it is for a professional to kill and get away with it. He can do it all right. You don't want that to happen, and neither do I. I admire your father tremendously. We need him and a thousand more like him if we're ever going to achieve a more peaceful world. And we can only do it by eliminating the scum that live by crime, starting at the top.'

Again he spoke as if it were a holy crusade. Could he really mean that? By his own admission he had, apparently, already killed people that he thought the world was well rid of. But where did it stop if not with his own destruction?

She tried to listen to the person behind the words, to persuade herself that people did not always mean what they said. But all she could hear was a man who had carried a gutful of fire inside him since he was thirteen years old, dedicated to carrying on his father's work of ridding the earth of evil as he saw it.

The one thing she was sure of was his respect and admiration of her own father. She picked up on the reasonable part of his remarks. 'You really do want to protect my father, don't you?' she said wonderingly, completely convinced now on that point.

'I do.' His voice and posture had softened a little 'So we need to play the game. I'm only sorry for your parents' suffering, thinking you in danger. But it won't be for long.'

'What do they know?' She felt her heart contract with pain for their anguish.

'I had to make it look like a real kidnaping, because the killer and I are supposed to be working together. So I had to get you out of the picture. Then, when your folks got back on the ship, thinking you were following on a later tender, they received a message telling them that you were being held for one million dollars ransom, and giving them directions for leaving it.'

'A million dollars!' she gasped.

Heinsohn shrugged. 'I know. It's rough. But your father is a wealthy man, and with his contacts here in Alaska he shouldn't have too hard a time raising that amount. Anyway, we have a good chance of retrieving the money once I remove the threat to his life for good.' He grinned then, a humorless, sardonic grin. 'Maybe your father will give me a reward when I return his daughter safely.' He sobered immediately. 'I'm joking, of course. He must not know until he's safely back home how you got back. He'll ask, of course, but you'll have to convince him that *you're* still in danger while still on the ship. He'll pay more attention to that than a threat to his own life.

'You won't see me again after I get you back on board,' he continued, 'but you can be sure I'll be there, waiting for the right time. Of course, if you decide to have me found so the "kidnaper" can be brought to justice, that will sign your father's death warrant. Neither of us wants that.'

Leonie's mind seemed to spin. Not one, but two professional killers on board ship with whom they'd been associating! After a lifetime of mingling with law enforcement people and the cultured, gentle word of music, it seemed incredible to her that she could be collaborating with a criminal. It was all part of unreality of the scene. But what choice did she have? 'You know I won't do anything to jeopardize my father's safety,' she said shortly.

A sudden thought struck her. 'It just occurred to me—this is why you backed out of your part in "The Shooting of Dan McGrew" for the Talent Show!'

Caught off base, he threw her a startled glance as wild-eyed as a horse spooked by an apparition. She thought bewilderedly: what did I say? But he recovered quickly and said evenly, 'Sure. I knew I'd have to be out of sight when we got back to the ship. Remember, I *know* when the attempt on your father's life will be made. Try to enjoy the rest of the cruise and not let anything spoil it for you. The judge will be safe. I promise you.'

'The ransom will have to be paid in Anchorage, won't it?'

'Yes. That's where we're headed now. We'll spend the night at a campground there and wait for the ship to arrive.' He hadn't missed the quick involuntary look she darted at him as he spoke. 'I'll sleep in the bunk over the cab and you can get back where you were before,' he said blandly, as if it were the most natural thing for them to be together like this. 'There's a nylon carryall stashed away somewhere back there,' he went on, 'and I think you'll find everything you need to be comfortable.'

She shivered a little to think how carefully it had all been planned and thought out—the advance furnishing and availability of the camper, which had to involve a third party, the whole thing choreographed like a ballet.

Something else occurred to her. 'Where is the ransom supposed to be paid?'

'Earthquake Park.'

CHAPTER NINETEEN

ESCALATE...
to increase or intensify.

'"The Chena arrived at Valdez at 16:12 hours, March 27. About 17:31 o'clock, while discharging cargo, we felt a severe earthquake followed almost immediately by tidal waves. There were very heavy shocks about every half minute. Mounds of water were hitting at us from all directions. I was in the dining room. I made it to the bridge (three decks up) by climbing a vertical ladder. God knows how I got there.

'"The Valdez piers started to collapse right away. There was a tremendous noise. The ship was laying over to port. I had been in earthquakes before, but I knew right away that this was the worst one yet. The Chena raised about 30 feet on an oncoming wave. The whole ship listed and heeled to port about 50 degrees. Then it was slammed down heavily on the spot where the docks had disintegrated moments before. I saw people running—with no place to run to. It was just ghastly. They were just engulfed by buildings, water, mud, and everything. The Chena dropped where the people had been. That is what has kept me awake for days.

There was no sight of them. We stayed there momentarily. Then there was an ungodly backroll to starboard. Then she came upright. Then we took another heavy roll to port.

'"I could see the land (at Valdez) jumping and leaping in a terrible turmoil. We were inside of where the dock had been. We had been washed into where the small boat harbor used to be. There was no water under the Chena for a brief interval. I realized we had to get out quickly if we were ever going to get out at all. There was water under us again. The stern was sitting in broken piling, rocks, and mud.

'"I signaled to the engine room for power and got it very rapidly. I called for 'slow ahead' then 'half ahead' and finally for 'full.' In about four minutes, I would guess, we were moving appreciably, scraping on and off the mud (bottom) as the waves went up and down. People ashore said they saw us slide sideways off a mat of willow trees (placed as part of the fill material in the harbor) and that helped us put our bow out. We couldn't turn. We were moving along the shore, with the stern in the mud. Big mounds of water came up and flattened out. Water inshore was rushing out. A big gush of water came off the beach and hit the bow and swung her out about 10 degrees. If that hadn't happened, we would have stayed there with the bow jammed in a mud bank and provided a new dock for the town of Valdez! We broke free. The bow pushed through the wreckage of a cannery. We went out into the bay and had to stop. The condensers were plugged with mud and pieces of the dock. The chief mate, Neal L. Larsen, checked to see then if we were taking water. We were taking none. It was unbelievable after what the ship had been through. We had the lifeboats all manned and ready. I didn't think she would float in deep water. Maybe the soft mud bottom made the diference.'"

'Whew!' said Charlie Beardsley. 'That was quite a story.'

'Wasn't that a fantastic account?' Professor Barnes' gray eyes glowed with the enthusiasm he always generated when passing on information that fascinated him. Then, suddenly, his eyes filled with pain, and his audience knew he was remembering something that distressed him deeply. Evidently he had a poignant memory of his own about the tremendous quake.

'Who was that talking?' Charlie wanted to know.

'That was Captain M.D. Stewart, Master of the vessel, the Chena, recording the events of March 27, 1964. The shaking only lasted about four minutes, but over one hundred people lost their lives, and of course many homes and businesses were destroyed. On the north side of Fourth Avenue, between A and

E Streets, stores were dropped from ten to twelve feet.'

'Well, that sure was an interesting reading,' Charlie said again, savoring his early morning coffee on the Prom Deck. 'I'm sorry the Warwicks missed it. They seem to set store by things like that. Where do you suppose they all got to? They've been right here every other morning. And I haven't seen Miss Leonie since she got off the tender in Homer. Not sick, is she? We did have a whole day and night at sea.'

'I really don't know,' answered Barnes, 'but I hope that's not the case.'

Charlie took another sip of his coffee, cocked an eye at a sweet roll, then felt the roll at his waistline with a pudgy hand. After a long moment he rolled his eyes heavenward and gave up the fight. 'Ummm. Good! Ah,' he continued, ignoring his mouthful, 'here's someone who should know where she is.'

Irish, joining the little group, assured them he hadn't seen Leonie either since she had disembarked in Homer. He seemed quite uptight about it, but Barnes put that down to his annoyance at her having spent so much time in the other man's company. It amused him to see them paying court to her while she kept a cool distance, playing one against the other, obviously enjoying their company. Quite a girl, that.

Leonie, at that moment, was waking up in the pickup-camper.

Heinsohn informed her, 'I picked this camper park because it's close to Earthquake Park. If all goes well, you'll soon be back with your folks.'

After washing up as best she could and fortified by a hearty breakfast prepared on a small butane stove, Leonie felt more ready to cope. She wished they could have gone somewhere to eat, or at least gotten out of the camper for some fresh air, but he insisted they should not be seen outside now that they were in Anchorage. It was odd, she thought, how quickly a woman was demoralized by the lack of soap and hot water. She supposed it was food that did it for a man.

*   *   *

Back at the ship, they had waited for the tide to go out so the gangplank would not be at too steep an angle, then trooped off to take a bus tour of the city. Barnes, taking advantage of his height, turned from Charlie, sitting next to him, to crane his neck to look for the Warwicks. Not on this bus and, he was quite sure, not on any of the others. They all had to leave the ship by the same gangplank and he had watched for them very carefully. He was sure he couldn't have missed them. How very strange. He felt an odd sense of disappointment. Usually they maneuvered to get a position near him when he was explaining something. Not only was it flattering, but he truly appreciated people with inquiring minds who were eager to learn all they could even on vacation, and whose pleasure was intensified by knowledge of the people and customs of a new locale.

The bus followed Ocean Dock Drive to the Captain Cook Memorial in Resolution Park. There was an impressive bronze statue of Captain James Cook, the Yorkshire farmhand's son who had gone on to the Royal Navy and honors. He gazed out over the waters of Cook Inlet—waters he had charted when his boats 'Resolution' and 'Discovery' had been dispatched to examine the arm leading to the east. Disappointed because the estuary was a dead end instead of leading to the Northwest Passage as he had hoped, Cook named it River Turnagain. Difficult to navigate, the early explorers had to 'turn again' and again, to keep from running aground. About twenty years after Cook, Captain Vancouver renamed it Turnagain Arm.

As the group stood on the wooden deck of the memorial, enjoying a beautiful view of Knik Arm and Mt. Susitna, known as Sleeping Lady, Dr. Barnes searched thoroughly once more for the Warwicks. They were not to be seen. A concerned frown wrinkled his agreeably homely face as he made his way back to the bus. He was convinced now that there was something wrong with Leonie.

As the bus turned onto Northern Lights Boulevard, the professor was distracted from his concern for the Warwicks by Charlie's myriad questions. Ordinarily it gave him great pleasure to educate people on the wonders of Alaska, particularly those around Anchorage, his home town. But now he wore an air of detachment, his answers almost perfunctory as he informed Charlie that the thirty-foot-plus tides of Turnagain Arm and Cook Inlet were second only to those in the Bay of Fundy in Novia Scotia, and that although Alaska was larger than Texas, it had fewer miles of road than Connecticut. He was relieved when the bus driver picked up the microphone and began his tour-guide spiel.

'You might like to know where Anchorage got its name,' the driver began. 'It was first called Woodrow and then Ship Creek'—he pronounced it 'Crick.' 'That was as far as the ships of the Pacific Steamship Line could go up Cook Inlet in the early years, and when they found the place offered decent anchorage to incoming vessels, the government put a post office there in 1915 and had the place called Anchorage.

'It's not unusual to see aircraft from all over the world here,' he continued. 'That's because flights between Europe and Asia and vice versa stop to refuel here. There are two interconnected lakes—Hood and Spenard—just north of Anchorage International Airport, and they house more small aircraft than any other airbase in the world. There are more than fifty air taxi companies here. In the winter, many small planes switch to skiis from floats and wheels. So you see, where you have parking lots in the Lower 48, we have parking *lakes*!

'Of course, there are other differences.' A note of mischief crept into his voice. 'The philosophy of the area is expressed in a bumper sticker which reads: "We don't give a damn how they do it Outside!"'

Then he turned the laughter back at himself when he went on, 'Cook Inlet inhabitants are unique. They've been described as "a marvelous collection of mavericks, dreamers, nuts and utter damn fools unmatched anywhere in the world."'

With Beardsley silent during the driver's lecture, Barnes' thoughts turned once more to the Warwicks. All this information was old hat to him anyway. He was anxious to find out what had happened to Leonie. He made up his mind right then that if he had somehow missed them and they showed up in Earthquake Park, he would join them there.

Perhaps he could learn something about this mystifying situation. Even if Leonie were sick and confined to the ship, she simply would not allow her parents to stay aboard with her and miss the tour. And, surely, if she were taken seriously ill they would have heard, wouldn't they? He cut off his disturbed thoughts as the guide began to speak again.

'You've heard about our famous tides that can go as high as thirty-nine feet. Anchorage is not an ice-free port, but the tides are so high and fast they keep the ice broken up. We also have something called a Bore Tide. It's something the locals learn early on not to play with, and sometimes brings grief to a newcomer.

'Actually, we have two a day in Turnagain Arm—at the two low tides of each twenty-four-hour cycle. They're caused primarily by the funneling of tide water into the narrower, high-walled area of the Inlet. The biggest of them comes at the time of the full and new moon. And if the famous Turnagain Wind from the southwest, what we call "The Cannon," is blowing against the water, it holds it back to create an even higher wall.

'In August of 1980, there was a headline in the *Anchorage Times* which read: "Bore Tides surging danger in Cook Inlet." They went on to tell how a small wave, only about knee-high, upended a sixteen-ton surplus

208

landing craft, a tracked amphibious vehicle that someone was playing with on the mud flats. And earlier, a State Park Ranger saw a big bull moose ambling by the water's edge along Cook Inlet, around Bird Point, as a Bore Tide about six feet high approached at about ten knots. When the water was about 250 yards away, the moose heard the big roar and began to run. He stayed ahead a while, then the wave caught up. It didn't knock him down. It didn't need to. There simply was too much water and it was too cold. That huge animal was overwhelmed in five minutes.' His smile was a bit grim now. 'So you won't play in the mud while you're here, will you?'

Everyone was laughing as they pulled up at Earthquake Park, but Barnes' brow was still creased in a way that was not characteristic.

Looking down at the softball fields, it was hard to imagine the earth convulsing as it had that terrible Good Friday of 1964, leaving 135 acres of desolation in this place alone. But the evidence was there in the steep drop-off before them, and in the tortured mounds of earth thrown up like ocean waves, still a gripping sight in spite of the smoothing influence of time.

Barnes, recalling the thirty-foot crevasses that engulfed people, cars, and buildings, shuddered as he relived again the nightmare of whole streets cracking open or sliding into the sea. The bluffs along the shore on the

209

west side of the city, where the group now stood, were especially vulnerable because it was here that an abundance of Bootlegger Cove blue clay surfaced. In areas where this was concentrated, the earth compacted with the awful shaking and reacted something like a horizontal landslide, with the most slippage along the saturated clay up to the nearest unconfined edge.

Now, more than twenty years later, Barnes trembled, remembering that while he was away, his wife watched their two small boys disappear from their own front yard as the earth opened up and swallowed them whole. She had to be institutionalized, and would remain so for the rest of her life. His pain had lessened now, but he had to steel himself to stand with the others and read the memorial plaque which detailed that terrible day. When he turned away, the Warwicks were there.

He almost gaped in his astonishment. 'Why, I thought you'd missed the tour!' he exclaimed as he hurried toward them. 'And where's Leonie? I hope she's not ill.'

John Warwick controlled his voice so fiercely it was almost a monotone. 'She's been ... detained,' he said finally.

Detained? The word struck Barnes as an odd thing to say. And why did Sanna look as though she was about to cry? Courtesy forbade his pursuing the subject further, so he turned the conversation to less personal channels. But it was obvious the usually attentive Warwicks were not hearing a word. He remained thoughtful, convinced there was something very strange afoot.

CHAPTER TWENTY

ACCELERATE...
to increase the speed of.

The next thing Morton Barnes knew, the Warwicks were not even beside him, but standing by the side of the road looking anxiously in all directions. What an odd turn of events! Only now did he make a conscious note of the large blue tote bag that the judge carried slung over one shoulder. Surely they hadn't spent the morning shopping when there were sights to be seen! As he watched, Sanna, looking paler and more tearful than ever, whispered something to her husband. He nodded gravely, then lowered the outsized bag to the ground at some distance from himself.

As Barnes tried to make sense of these strange actions, two astonishing things happened. Seemingly out of nowhere, a small man, his face obscured by a smoky-dark visor, roared by on a Honda, scooped up the tote and *varoomed* away before anyone realized what was happening.

Moments later, as the startled crowd chattered and exclaimed excitedly over what they took to be a theft, a wild-eyed Leonie came running down the road to hurl herself into her parents' arms. Her mouth worked with emotion, and it took every ounce of self-control for her to keep from howling and bursting into tears. Sanna, also wide-eyed, but containing her tears, was trembling from head to foot.

Barnes was the only one close enough to hear John Warwick say, low-voiced but savagely, 'Who was it, Leonie? Did you know who it was?' The professor, ignorant of Leonie's kidnaping, thought in bewilderment: how can Leonie be expected to know a local thief? Leonie only had time to answer shakily, 'We can't talk now, Dad. Later. But I'm all right, truly I am.' Then they were surrounded by a buzzing crowd, eager to relive the drama of a bold daylight robbery.

As the driver herded them back to the bus, the Warwicks did their best not to call attention to themselves and to act as naturally as possible, but each gripped one of Leonie's hands very hard. The big Irishman, Barnes noted, looked as though he wanted to do the same. And where, he wondered suddenly, had *he* come from? Everyone seemed to be appearing out of thin air this morning!

That afternoon, as they boarded a different bus for another tour, Barnes was relieved to see the Warwicks quite themselves again. Only Leonie was still a little white and strained-looking, but apparently she'd had some sort of setback so that was to be expected. He noted too that the big Irishman had managed to get a seat next to her and was now openly holding her hand. The huge blond man who also vied for her attention was not on the bus. Ah, romance! thought the professor, a bit wistfully.

Pat, their red-headed and ebullient bus driver, was bright, knowledgeable and had obviously researched much of the area's history. He was also quite a wit. They enjoyed his stories as they exclaimed over the beautifully-kept grounds of the University of Alaska. They exclaimed even more over the $900,000 solid jade staircase in the Sheraton Hotel, which reputedly glowed in the dark. And they laughed at his jokes as they traveled the Seward Highway southward into the Kenai Mountains. They sobered somewhat as they came to Turnagain Arm and Pat pointed out an area on the left known as Potter's Marsh, now a bird sanctuary, where the earth sank ten to twelve feet in the Good Friday earthquake. But they were soon laughing again as he referred to the glacial silt creating a problem in Alaska's rivers and inlets as 'too thick to drink and too thin to plow!'

He pointed out the incredible slopes of the great peaks known as Suicide Peaks, and informed them that the fireweed leaves would turn bright orange in the fall, while snowfall might be as early as the first of September. Residents still called the first flurries of snow in the early fall 'termination dust,' so named by the old-time prospectors who saw the winter's snow putting an end to their summer mining activities.

Pat pointed out more of the big-leafed, incredibly thorny Devil's Club they had seen so much of on the Mendenhall Float Trip, explaining that it had once been used in a form of exorcism by the Indians, who believed the evil spirits escaped through the puncture wounds. And he was openly proud of the beauties of his state as they toured the Alyeska Ski Resort, the largest and only year-round area.

But the highlight of his one-man show was a marvelous, letter-perfect recitation of Robert W. Service's classic poem, 'The Cremation of Sam McGee.' When he had acknowledged the wild applause, he told them, 'When we get to Fourth and C Streets, you'll see a representation of another classic by Robert Service, "The Shooting of Dan McGrew."'

As they passed the mural depicting the famous poem, on the outside of the Malamute Saloon, Leonie was reminded that their own rendition of it was only a day and a half away. Apparently Irish was thinking the same thing, for he turned to her and grinned. 'Are you feeling all right now?' he asked. 'We want "the lady that's known as Lou" in tiptop shape tomorrow night.'

'I'm fine, thank you,' Leonie replied, and reluctantly wrenched her eyes away from the compelling blue gaze. For the first time since her kidnaping she gave thought to her appearance. I'm going to have to do something about this hair before the Talent Show, she thought, then decided if she could worry about that, she was back to normal.

*　　*　　*

Returning from the beauty shop below decks the next morning, Leonie took a wrong turn and suddenly found herself in the crew's quarters. The sign identifying the area made it plain she was not welcome. Passengers were not allowed there.

As she began a hasty retreat around the nearest corner, her movement was arrested by the sound of voices coming from a half-opened door. As she quickly ducked back out of sight, two things aroused her curiosity enough to make her linger a moment. Not only were the men speaking in conspiratorial tones, but they were speaking in English. The crew spoke Chinese. As one of them stepped out into the passageway, the lowered voice of the man still inside the room could be clearly heard. 'No sir! We agreed on a price, Sam, and that's all you get. Dammit, man! All you have to do is spend one night in the sick bay. That's no big deal. And you damn well better keep your mouth shut!'

Leonie's eyes widened in shock. Heinsohn! Unmistakably.

Peeking out, she could barely suppress a gasp of surprise as the familiar face of their steward, Sam, came fully into view. Fortunately, he turned his back on her and headed the other way.

Leonie fled back to less sinister surroundings after some more wrong turning, reviewing what she had just heard. 'You won't see me again after we get back to the ship,' Heinsohn had said. And when she'd asked why they had a new steward that morning, was told that Sam was sick. It made sense now. Obviously, the steward had been bribed to let Heinsohn hide out in his cabin while he spent the night in sick bay under some pretext or another. No one would think of checking a supposedly empty steward's cabin.

She longed to tell her father what she'd seen, but he was the very one she couldn't confide in. She'd had a hard enough time convincing him it was not safe for her to say anything at all about her kidnaping until they were safely home. She knew she could not lie convincingly about not knowing her abductor, and so let the judge think that she was the one still in danger. The ransom, she had told him earnestly, had paid for more than her return; it had also paid for her silence until the kidnaper could get safely away. The judge had to accept that, only insisting she not get out of sight for the remainder of the voyage. The beauty shop had seemed a safe enough destination.

'Just one night,' Heinsohn had told Sam. That must mean he was planning his move for the following day. Then, realization struck like lightning. That meant the killer was doing the same! Her pulses quickened, dread seizing her as she thought of the hours marching inexorably on to the moment when someone would try to murder her father. Heinsohn had been so confident, but could she be sure he would be successful in thwarting that attempt? One thing was reassuring. He was still there. He hadn't taken the money and run. Nothing she had said on that memorable ride out of Homer had swerved him from his stated purpose as an avenger.

'Oh, your hair is lovely, but your color's still not too good,' Sanna said worriedly as Leonie joined her parents on the Prom Deck later. 'How are you feeling?'

'Oh, I'm fine now, Mom,' Leonie said

hastily. 'I was pretty shaken up all day yesterday, I guess, but I'm fine now.' She knew it was terribly difficult for her parents to refrain from asking questions about what had happened on that unbelievable day in Homer.

They were relaxing once more in their deck chairs when Mrs. Courtland, whom Sanna still called the Duchess, came up with the Carrascos in tow. Luis did not look at all well, Leonie noticed, and felt sorry for poor Maribel who kept darting worried glances at him. He had little to say, letting Maribel do most of the talking, with the Duchess translating to include the rest of the group in the conversation. Maribel had lost most of her shyness and was almost vivacious now that she could chatter freely in Spanish.

'Maribel says they're getting excited about the Talent Show performance tomorrow night,' Mrs. Courtland said. 'She has her costume all ready.' The Duchess made a determined effort not to show her own anxiety about the unusually quiet Luis. She knew that although his condition had worsened in the last few days he was adamant in refusing to curtail his activities. 'He prefers to do all those things we had planned,' Maribel had told her tearfully earlier in the day, 'rather than take care of himself and perhaps have a little more . . .'—she choked on the word—'time.'

'We have a saying in English,' the Duchess had told the weeping girl gently, 'to the effect that *la calidad*, the quality of life, is more important than *la cantidad*, the amount of it. Luis seems to agree, and you would want it so for his sake, wouldn't you?' Maribel, choked with sorrow, could only nod dumbly.

The Carrascos did not stay long. 'I must prepare myself for our great performance,' Luis managed to smile, 'and get plenty of rest.' Leonie wondered why her mother and Mrs. Courtland looked so sad as they exchanged knowing glances.

They had just settled back after bidding the Carrascos good night, when Charlie bustled up, more popeyed than ever, his face an odd mixture of consternation, shock and self-importance.

'Say, have you heard?' He was practically squeaking with excitement. 'One of the crew has been murdered—stabbed! Can you imagine! His body was in one of the lifeboats. I had chased the Gibson kids up to the Boat Deck, because they'd run off with the last of the ping-pong balls again, and I was with them when they found him. They were playing hide-and-seek with me, and the poor kids are hysterical.' Charlie, now full of compassion, had been castigating the children earlier. 'Blasted teenagers! They've lost two volleyballs in the water, used a watermelon for a football, and now I can't play ping-pong.' But then he said again, 'Poor kids. A hell of a thing to happen to a couple of youngsters.'

As he spoke, a horrible suspicion was dawning in Leonie's mind. 'Did you know who it was?' she asked, and her father was the only one perceptive enough to wonder why that would be of interest to her.

She was not particularly surprised when Charlie answered, 'Absolutely. It was our own steward, Sam.'

CHAPTER TWENTY-ONE

CULMINATE...
to come to full effect; climax.

There was no way to keep the murder quiet. Not when the body had been discovered by some of the passengers. At lunchtime every table buzzed with it. People expressed horror, but were stimulated and titillated by the drama of violence that intruded into their pleasant cruise.

'Have you noticed,' Irish said to Leonie, with a trace of bitterness in his voice, 'how much less concerned people are with the misfortunes of others if those others happen to look different or speak another language? As if that made them less human! I actually heard one of our shipmates say, "No, not one of the passengers. It was only a steward!"'

Leonie studied him thoughtfully. It was no surprise to have him at their table again. Apparently he had made a permanent switch with the original occupant of his chair, and it was now taken for granted he would be there with them. A corner of her brain she tried to ignore kept talking to her. What do you really know about him? It's quite possible he's mixed up in all this, too. He has never even questioned your disappearance!

Something else occurred to her. He hadn't asked about Heinsohn! Surely he must have wondered why no one had seen him since Homer. Her parents had missed him immediately—(he'd been so much in evidence)—and she had had to evade, telling them he'd stayed in Homer on business, keeping her promise not to expose him as yet. She had firmly refused to explain how she had 'escaped' and gotten back to Anchorage, promising a full revelation later. But Irish had shown no curiosity about any of this. It seemed inconceivable.

Then color flooded her cheeks, and she was thankful he was looking the other way. Could he assume that she and Heinsohn had had an intimate interlude in Homer, away from the scrutiny of family and shipmates?

The part of her mind that would not listen to feelings spoke again. 'But there's another

221

reason: he might have known about the kidnaping all along! Maybe he and Heinsohn were in this together, making a pretense of not liking each other as they competed for your attentions.' Even as she tried to ignore that train of thought again, she remembered the time she had caught the two men unaware, talking secretively. She recalled their guilty start and the glib, plausible explanation that they were plotting something for the Talent Show and wanted to involve her. But even then she had been conscious of deep, dark currents under the superficial behavior.

It was all so puzzling. There was no doubt Irish had changed in the few days since Heinsohn had disappeared. She had the strange impression that he had dropped a part he no longer needed to play. She had noted once before that he had been at his boldest and brashest when Heinsohn was present. A smoke screen?

She questioned her mother after lunch, as they made final preparations for their Talent Show performance.

'Oh, yes,' Sanna said. 'Of course Irish asked about you. As soon as it was obvious you hadn't come back with us from Homer. Your father told him quite truthfully you'd missed the last tender, then later made up a story about your renting a car and catching up with us in Anchorage. I guess he thought you'd gone off with Werner Heinsohn, because his face was a thundercloud as I spoke. And it did seem a logical conclusion when you both disappeared at once. Of course, we knew better than that.'

Even now Sanna had a questioning look, and Leonie knew her parents, too, must think it a strange coincidence that she and Heinsohn would fall out of sight at the same time by accident. But she had to keep him above suspicion in her kidnaping until he had removed the menace of Petrosino's henchman, assigned to kill her father.

'You know,' Sanna began, 'that was a funny thing, your appearing out of the blue like that in Earthquake Park. We never did see...'

Leonie interrupted her, quickly and firmly. 'Mom, we really can't discuss all that now. Remember? Be patient a little longer. Now tell me, what do you think of my outfit?' And she changed the subject deftly as they continued working on the costumes.

Her tension grew steadily throughout the afternoon. It was doubly hard to bear because she could not share her anxiety with anyone. Her father noticed it, but misunderstood the cause. 'Not still nervous, are you, honey? I hope you're not worrying about the money I lost. I'd give everything I own to keep you safe. You know that.'

She squeezed his arm without answering,

so he continued. 'And please don't worry that I'll do something foolish. It does gall me terribly to sit back and do nothing while your kidnaper is loose. But if I have to wait to get some information from you until we get home, and he's safely hidden out in another country, then that's what I'll do for your protection.'

Leonie thought wildly; but how do we protect *you*? I can't do a thing but trust in Heinsohn to eliminate the threat to your life. There's simply no one else to turn to.

Keeping her knowledge to herself was almost more than she could bear. As Irish approached their deck chairs later, his powerful body a study in disciplined strength, she had an almost uncontrollable desire to jump up and throw herself into his arms, spilling the entire story. As she fought her runaway emotions, a feeling of utter desolation overcame her. Flanked by her loving parents and surrounded by a ship full of people, she still had that terrible hollow feeling of aloneness, of yearning for a special person to care for, who would care about her. She knew it was this very thing she had to fight when the powerful pull of Irish's attraction overcome her almost against her will. She just had to make sure who and what he really was.

He, watching her keenly, well aware of how tense she was, felt an almost irresistible urge to gather her in and hold her close, soothing and smoothing that beautiful bright head. His own guilty knowledge clamored to burst forth. But a muscle twitching in his jaw was the only sign of his inner turmoil as he held out a hand and drew her to her feet. 'Let's go for a walk. Dr. Barnes is expounding on the outside deck again, and we can go and get educated to take our minds off the show tonight. I guess I've been having opening-night jitters, although I suppose you're used to performing before large groups of people with all your piano concerts.'

Leonie obediently allowed herself to be led outside to where Barnes' usual group of admirers had gathered, but her mind spun crazily. How did Irish know she was a concert pianist? Could her parents have told him? She barely heard Barnes as he held forth on his pet peeve: misconceptions about Alaska.

'But, Charlie,' he was remonstrating, 'Alaska has cattle country too. The Aleutian Chain and Kodiak Island have many miles of beautiful grasslands. And our Matanuska Valley, Mat-Su as we call it, is Alaska's bread basket. World record vegetables. If you have a cabbage the size of a basketball, it's considered the runt of the litter. And take Barrow, for instance. It's our northernmost city and the largest Eskimo community in the world. But do you find igloos all over the place? No. You have new apartments with heat, running water, and inside plumbing. And you have the Top of the World Hotel, open year-round, with conference and banquet facilities.

'It distresses me when people think of Alaska as nothing but a perpetually frozen, barren wasteland,' he continued. 'I'm sure it annoys you if people come to Texas, which is full of forests, lakes and mountains, expecting only cowboys and Indians on a flat, treeless plain. The point is, there *are* such things, but they don't represent the entire state.'

'Maybe they're not as ignorant as they sound,' Charlie grinned. 'Maybe it's just pure cussedness, and they talk that way just to get a rise out of you.'

Barnes' irritation left him immediately. 'Only you would think of that, Charlie!' He laughed as he got to his feet.

'I love Alaska,' Charlie said, serious now. 'I'd retire here if I could strike it rich—oil, gold, whatever.'

'What you need,' Barnes teased him, 'is to put your money on the Tanana Ice Pool and guess what month, day, hour and minute you think the ice will move out of the Tanana River. Even if the money is divided between several winners, individuals may win as much as $50,000.'

As the group broke up, laughing, Barnes spied Irish and Leonie. 'Ah! Here come our thespians. Is your soon-to-be-prize-winning act still a big secret to all but a favored few?'

'Yes,' Leonie answered. 'We thought it would be more fun if people didn't know what we were presenting beforehand. Will we see you there?'

'Front row center. I wouldn't miss it for anything!'

And there he was when the foot-tapping strains of 'Maple Leaf Rag' signalled the start of their performance.

The music faded as Irish started to read. '"*A bunch of the boys were whooping it up in the Malamute Saloon,*"' he began in his rich, deep-chested baritone. '"*The kid that handles the music box was hitting a rag-time tune. / Back of the bar, in a solo game, sat Dangerous Dan McGrew.*"'

Once more the rousing notes of the 'William Tell Overture,' made their identification of 'Dangerous Dan' as Luis leered at Leonie and made larger-than-life gestures with his card playing.

'"*And watching his luck,*"' Irish continued with his recitation, '"*was his light-of-love, the lady that's known as Lou.*"' Sanna slipped into the strains of that old tear-jerker, 'She's Only a Bird in a Gilded Cage,' as Leonie fluttered her extravagant eyelashes and leaned familiarly over Luis. She had borrowed an elaborate wig and made an alluring picture in her Gay nineties costume with its ruffled skirt and wasp waist.

Next followed Irish's dramatic rendition of the entrance of 'The Stranger' as Sanna played some of the more sinister passages of 'The Erl King.' Her artistry at the piano, coupled with Irish's memorable voice, had a spellbinding effect. Leonie could feel herself caught up in the mood of suspense as a mysterious apparition, looking more dead than alive, stumbled *'out of the night, which was fifty below'* into the noisy saloon to empty his poke—his bag of gold—on the bar. She could feel the tension of the scene as the narrator in the poem, describing the electrifying effect of the stranger on the group, began to suspect who he might be and to wonder what he might do next.

The script called for 'The Stranger' to stumble over to the piano when 'The Kid' left to have a drink. But, since the judge's musical repertoire reached no higher than 'Chopsticks,' Sanna continued to play and he went through the motions, while the audience roared at the poem's description of his marvelous skill at the piano.

The music, as described by Irish's eloquent reading, evoked the hunger and loneliness of a man who had left everything to search for gold, when the woman he loved spurned him to take up with the man who had already struck it rich.

Then the music changed as the reading revealed his thwarted longings for the home and true love denied him, and his thirst for vengeance. It had softened and almost died away as the poem described 'The Stranger's' years of loneliness and despair, then built to a stirring crescendo as it spoke of his remembrance of an ancient wrong and the lust to kill.

Leonie felt a shivering thrill up her spine as Irish's hypnotic voice, interpreting the music, now thundered ... '"*and it seemed to say, Repay, Repay, and my eyes were blind with blood!*"'

The music, which had built to an unbearable peak of emotion, stopped with a deafening crash, and Leonie was astonished to find herself so carried away that she actually jumped. She could see by their expressions that the others were equally caught up in the spell, and for a moment not a sound could be heard.

Then the reading continued as 'The Stranger' spoke to the group in the saloon, identifying 'Dan McGrew' as the root of the injustice dealt him and the target of his vengeance. Irish's voice spotlighted the culprit in menacing tones. '"*One of you is a hound of hell ... and that one is Dan McGrew!*"' And Sanna played 'Dangerous Dan's' theme in a wailing minor key, hinting at what was to come.

The next few seconds were startling in their intensity, especially after the complete immobility of the players. As Irish's voice rang out, describing the action, the lights suddenly went out, and a woman screamed shrilly as two loud reports split the darkness, echoed by the sudden crashing of chairs on the floor. The lights came on then to reveal that *'two men lay stiff and stark.'*

Crouched as she was over her father, playing 'The Stranger,' several heart-stopping seconds had passed before Leonie realized that the script was not progressing as it should. Irish was supposed to continue with the words *'"Pitched on his head, and pumped full of lead, was Dangerous Dan McGrew. / While the man from the creeks was clutched to the breast of the lady that's known as Lou."'*

Leonie risked a glance upward just as the screaming started in earnest, but her brain would not acknowledge what her eyes were relaying.

Sanna, at the side of the stage, could not see all that went on, and continued with the mournful notes of Chopin's 'Funeral March,' providing a fitting background for a horrifying scene.

Luis lay very still, pitched forward almost close enough to touch Leonie, but it was not until she struggled to her feet in bewilderment, wondering what had gone wrong, that she saw the bullet hole and the blood pouring from his back. Maribel was on stage by now, cradling Luis' head in her arms.

The judge, white-faced, was on his feet too, all of them staring toward the back of the stage where the curtains had parted and Irish was now crouched over another figure, gun in hand.

Leonie was confused. Irish wasn't supposed to have a gun! And who was the extra person? The fog of confusion parted with horrible clarity as she came close enough to see the face of the unexpected man who lay on his back with a terrible wound in his chest. Werner Heinsohn! And Irish—no doubt of it—had just killed him!

Her worst fears were realized. Irish was the man sent to kill her father! And he had just killed the man who had tried to protect him.

It was too much. The room whirled around her and she fell away into unfathomable darkness.

CHAPTER TWENTY-TWO

TERMINATE...
to bring to a conclusion.

'How is Maribel?' Sanna asked.

'She's all right,' Mrs. Courtland sighed. 'Very sad, of course, but resigned and, I think, almost relieved. They were so in love, and she misses Luis desperately. But she says over and over again how merciful it was, since he couldn't live, that he could go so quickly, with no time for pain, and while he was enjoying life. You know how much fun he had at the rehearsal. She says he had an absolutely marvelous time being "Dangerous Dan McGrew." And she even said...'

The Duchess stopped abruptly, choked on a sob, and clutched Sanna's arm in a most uncharacteristic loss of control. When she could continue she gave a watery, apologetic smile and went on. 'She said she could just hear Luis telling everyone how lucky he was to die in the arms of *two* beautiful women! Can you imagine such bravery! Poor, poor child!' And then the Duchess broke down completely.

'What will she do now?' Sanna asked a little later, after Mrs. Courtland had recovered.

'Well, I moved her into my cabin last night after ... after all that, and I'm going to take her back to Mexico City, to her family. She can't talk to a soul here, of course ... relied on Luis for that. I'll see that she gets safely back home. I have nothing else to do. After that, who knows?'

Sanna's eyes grew misty as she looked ahead to the coming months, thinking of both Maribel and Leonie, two innocent women trying to pick up the pieces of their broken lives, through no fault of their own. She said slowly, 'She's young yet, and very lovely. Perhaps she can learn to love again.' But as she spoke of Maribel she had a sudden vision of Leonie, holding hands with Irish, and thought of her hopes for her daughter's future, dashed so cruelly now that the likable Irishman, a *murderer*, had been taken into custody by the captain.

They were repairing the ravages of their tears when word came for Sanna to join the rest of her family in the captain's quarters.

As the Warwicks crowded in, Leonie was astonished to see Irish there, obviously waiting for them. Wasn't he supposed to be locked up somewhere? She supposed they were summoned to be witnesses to the harrowing events of the prior evening.

She avoided his eyes, and pretended to look around the cabin with interest. While considerably larger than theirs, the quarters were by no means luxurious.

'Come in, come in!' Captain Grainger, offering seats and coffee, was a tall, spare, rather severe-looking man. But his face was transformed as he smiled and twinkled at the ladies. 'No need to be nervous because I am not on the bridge,' he said. 'We have our competent helmsmen, and an automatic pilot.' Leonie wished he would stay so relaxed and charming, but supposed a look of stern command was necessary to a ship's captain.

'Or are you looking surprised because I am not Chinese?' He laughed outright at that. 'I have lived in China for years, and have no trouble communicating with the crew.' Then he sobered somewhat as he got down to the business at hand.

'First of all, I must tell you that I know all about Miss Warwick's kidnaping experience. And, I think, Judge, that I have something that belongs to you.' His smile grew a little wider as he moved toward a locker, enjoying the looks of mystification. 'I found this,' Captain Grainger went on to explain, 'when I was called to open the cabin and go through the effects of the murdered steward, whom you knew as Sam.' He smiled again at the exclamations of surprise when he brought forth the bright blue tote bag, still filled with the ransom money. 'I had no idea,' he continued, 'that Mr. Heinsohn was hiding in Sam's cabin, or that he was involved in the kidnaping.'

There was an involuntary gasp from Sanna and the hiss of suddenly indrawn breath from the judge. Leonie thought in astonishment: with Heinsohn dead, how do you know that now?

Thinking of Werner, she dared not look at his murderer or acknowledge the ache in her heart at his deception, because she knew that she had fallen in love. But previous surprises did not compare with what came next, as

234

Captain Grainger spoke again.

'Now, I must introduce you to someone.' He paused for effect, obviously enjoying his dramatic role, then gestured toward Irish with the flourish of a magician about to produce a rabbit out of a hat. 'This is not Mr. Tom Callahan, as you've been led to believe, but Mr. Christopher Culhane, agent of the Federal Bureau of Investigation. I think the story should be his from now on.'

The Warwicks were too astonished to speak. Leonie felt such a tidal wave of emotion overcome her she dared not look at the big Irishman yet. Her father was the first to break the crackling silence. 'My word! And I thought I had just figured out why you looked familiar to me. There were all sorts of mysterious goings-on to make me look at you twice, and I finally decided you were not who you said you were.'

'Absolutely right, sir,' Irish said with a smile.

'And absolutely wrong, too,' the judge grumbled. 'Because I was sure you were the real Tom Callahan, whom I had seen at the time of the Petrosino trial.'

'But you saw me there, too, sir, when I testified briefly.' Irish told him. 'Later I learned that Petrosino had broken out of jail and disappeared, presumably to die in a crash of his private plane in the mountains. I was in the area, on vacation, and got involved in the

235

investigation. I saw Tom Callahan, and knew he wouldn't be there unless it was on business for the mob. And I felt sure that business had to do with Petrosino's disappearance. If we hadn't gotten suspicious it would have ended there, but further investigation proved that the second body, found with that of Petrosino's private pilot, was not Petrosino's at all, but that of a rival mob leader who had been constantly at war with Petrosino's gang, and who had also disappeared.

'I followed Callahan back to the city and had him under surveillance, when he was shot down by the rival gang members who hoped that by eliminating him, with Petrosino gone, they'd gotten rid of their worst competition.

'Heinsohn was up here, setting things up for Leonie's "kidnaping," and apparently did not get the word of the attack on Callahan. Then Callahan died before I could get any information out of him.'

In a flash, Leonie's mind flew back to that traumatic day when she had closed the door on her life with Walter to embark on a new one, only to be met by the aftermath of a brutal gangland killing. Memory, dredged from the subconscious, made her certain beyond a doubt now that the startling blue eyes that now gripped hers were those of the same man who had looked at her, unseeing, through the window of an ambulance. She remembered the despair in his face. Now she understood it. Callahan had died without speaking. Then how ...? Her father voiced the question before she could.

'Then how did you learn of the plot against us?' the judge asked. 'Surely you didn't come here by coincidence?'

'Not at all, sir,' Irish replied. 'We'd heard rumors from the underworld that Petrosino's threat was not an idle one, that he definitely meant to take your life. What was frightening was that the rumors persisted after Petrosino was supposed to be dead. I was quite sure that Callahan had to be in on the deception. Someone had to retrieve Petrosino from those mountains and take him to his hiding place, and Callahan was his trusted first lieutenant. We knew Petrosino planned to retire and give the reins to Callahan anyway, and presumed he had given Callahan instructions for your murder, Judge. It was a bad moment for me when I thought Callahan's secret had died with him, for only he, Petrosino and Heinsohn knew the plan. But, on the way to the hospital, when he was past knowing anyone, he spoke to me. I don't know who he thought I was, but he made a desperate effort to get someone to remove the incriminating evidence when he said just one word before he died—"tape."'

Irish paused a moment, his expression somber, reliving those turbulent hours. 'I went back to his car,' he continued, 'and did find tapes in it, but they were just what they appeared to be: music. We searched his apartment, but there was nothing there. Yet I knew it had to be somewhere, so I went back to the mountain cabin where I'd seen Callahan alone and where we now know he picked Petrosino up. I didn't realize until later that Petrosino was hiding in the back of the jeep, out of sight, when I saw Callahan come down, apparently alone. But someone had surprised him there, and he left in such a hurry that he forgot the tape with his instructions. Petrosino had recorded the whole plan so that he could stay out of sight until they staged his death. Then, had he not survived his parachuting from the plane, which had been rigged to explode, Callahan would still have been able to carry on.

'When I found the tape I learned the details of Leonie's kidnaping and your proposed murder, sir. After Callahan died, I decided the best way to protect you was to impersonate him. As you've already noticed, I look enough like him for someone who didn't know us to be deceived by the general description.' He stopped again, to grin at Leonie. 'But it was awfully hard to remember to act like he would act.'

'You did come on pretty strong at first,' Leonie said, 'but I gradually began to realize that you acted obnoxiously only when Heinsohn was present. You were quite different when we were alone. I couldn't understand it.'

Irish's grin grew wider. 'I thought I had blown it back there on the first day, when I rescued you from your locked cabin, because I forgot all about acting like Callahan.' He turned to Sanna. 'And I thought I'd given myself away when you asked me one time if I'd been to Europe and I answered without thinking, 'Not really.' What I meant, of course, was that I'd been there on business, but had done no touring or sightseeing whatsoever. That would have been a little hard to explain.'

Captain Grainger asked, 'And you knew all along that Mr. Heinsohn had planned to murder Judge Warwick during the Talent Show performance, only to hit poor Mr. Carrasco by mistake?'

Irish shook his head. 'No, Captain. I confess that was a complete surprise to me, and we almost had a tragedy with that ready-made murder scene. Because, you see, *I* was the one supposed to murder the judge in my role of Callahan. Heinsohn was to do the kidnaping, get the rest of his pay, then leave the money for me to take back to Petrosino. I never expected him to doublecross Petrosino and plan to make off with the money himself. Petrosino had complete confidence in Heinsohn, but unable to kill the judge himself, would trust that part

239

of it to no one but Tom Callahan. Unfortunately, I relaxed when I thought Heinsohn had run off with the money, thinking the judge then to be safe.

'I hated to put all of you through that anguish of Leonie's apparent kidnaping and the ransom, but I knew Leonie would be quite safe with Heinsohn. Although I had a bad moment there in Homer when she went off alone with him. I had hoped to be within sight of them during the day and follow his actions. There was no point in confronting him early. I had no evidence of crime until Leonie got back.'

He stopped, shaking his head in bewilderment. 'I knew he didn't trust me for some reason, but I still can't explain why he would risk coming back to the ship to kill the judge himself. That couldn't be important to him; he did only what Petrosino paid him to do. And he had an impeccable reputation for doing just that.' He shook his head again. 'I just can't understand it.'

'I can,' Leonie said simply, and every sound in the room ceased at once. Her nerves were so taut she very nearly giggled and said, 'Close your mouth, Dad!' Instead, she gulped and repeated, 'I can. Werner told me. He thought he was killing you, Ir—' She stopped, a comical look crinkling her face. 'What do I call you now?'

'"Irish" will do,' he smiled. 'They really

do call me that. You say Heinsohn was actually aiming for me?'

Leonie nodded.

'But why? Did he suspect I wasn't Callahan?'

'Oh, no, not at all!' Leonie explained. 'You were the target because he thought you *were.* He thought he was killing Tom Callahan to avenge his own father's death at Petrosino's hands. But that's another story. He was going to steal the ransom money from Petrosino and return it to Dad after he killed "Callahan." Of course, I had no idea that was you. He thought he'd be killing the man who was the heir to Petrosino's criminal empire. Poor Luis. Werner had no way of knowing we'd decided Luis would take your place as "Dangerous Dan," so you could be the narrator. Apparently, Werner just hid behind the curtains and fired at the back of the figure that was dressed like "Dan." He simply assumed it was you.'

'Imagine shooting an unarmed man in the back like that!' the judge exclaimed indignantly. 'It's frightening to think a man can be pleasant, attractive, and completely acceptable socially, yet be capable of an act like that. What darkness lies hidden in the depths of those twisted souls!'

'He was twisted in his thinking, Dad,' Leonie said sadly. 'He'd been warped by a personal tragedy early in life and honestly

241

thought he was doing the right thing. You know, I'm sorry for him.'

Sanna was scandalized. 'You can say that, after all you've been through? The man was nothing but a gangster, a gun for hire! There was probably nothing he would have stopped at if the price had been right.'

Leonie said evenly, 'I can't agree with you there, Mother. Sad to say, you're right about everything he did, but as for that last—well, you're just all wrong. By his own twisted logic he thought he was improving his world by eliminating evil—saw himself as some sort of avenging angel. And, in his own way, he lived by a very strict code.'

'I confess, I don't understand you, Leonie!' Sanna was almost angry. 'This was no Robin Hood!'

'But actually, Mother, in a way he was. He saw himself as the champion of justice. And justice, to him at least, was ridding the world of the criminal element who took his idolized father's life. He saw our judicial system as completely ineffective and corrupt. He heard his father agonize over the rulings that hamstrung law enforcement officers while they protected the rights of the very people who allowed their innocent victims no rights at all. It made no sense to him. It makes no sense to me, for that matter.'

She stopped and hastily held up a placating hand, noticing the expression on her father's face. 'I know, I know, Dad. I know exactly what you're thinking. And I don't want to start a discussion now as to why it's bad and dangerous for people to take the law into their own hands. I just want to say that I couldn't help but admire his dedication to his ideal, misguided or not. And that for all his dark deeds, there was something in him, some rare quality, that made me like him in spite of everything he'd done. Aside from the fact that he treated me with the utmost courtesy and respect.'

Sanna was thoughtful. 'Well, it's true there are strange things in life. There are mysterious forces and influences of which we are ignorant, that govern us even without our knowing it. We use words like "personality" and "body chemistry" and talk about "Fate" and "Providence" and coincidence. People who believe as we do often see the hand of God in inexplicable circumstances. Who knows, there may have been some purpose of His in having this man's life cross ours.'

'I hope you can believe that, Mother. I'd like to think that because of the time we spent together, even under those circumstances, we were able to add something to each other's lives. He certainly needed someone to confide in when he'd been carrying such a crushing burden of hatred around all these years.'

She repeated then, very briefly, the essence of what Heinsohn had told her concerning his background. When she'd finished, she said again softly, 'Poor Luis. He was just in the wrong place at the wrong time.'

'Don't grieve for Luis,' Sanna said. 'I can tell you this now. His quick death was really a blessing because he had only a short time to live.' Her family stared in surprise as she explained. 'It's Maribel I'm sorry for.'

The women were on the verge of tears, so Captain Grainger hastily steered the conversation into calmer waters. 'And how long have you been with the FBI, Mr. Culhane?'

'About ten years now, but I've only been working outside of the Lower 48 for the last couple of years.' He slid a sudden sideward glance at Leonie. 'Since my wife died in a car accident.'

There was an awkward silence, and again it was Captain Grainger who avoided the rocks like the good skipper he was, and navigated toward safer channels. 'One thing I can't understand,' he said, 'is how Mr. Heinsohn got a gun past customs and airport security.'

'He told me about that, too,' Leonie replied. 'He thought it was funny. He pretended to be an injured football player, and had a pair of wooden crutches specially made to accommodate the parts of his gun. As huge as he was, no one questioned an outsized pair of crutches. It never occurred to anyone to X-ray *crutches*.

244

'Later, he laughed at the thought of his having a real gun for the play when the others were acting with toy ones. It was awful to know he was planning to kill a man, but I couldn't say anything because even if I had known who that man was, I would have risked Dad's life by speaking out. It was either be quiet and let him eliminate the murderer, or let that murderer kill Dad. If I had only known who you were!' There was anguish in the look she threw Irish, and he was beside her in three quick strides. Without a trace of selfconsciousness he drew her into the circle of his arms and held her close against him.

Captain Grainger smiled benignly on them and cleared his throat to get their attention. 'I hope you can put the tragedy aside for the moment and enjoy the rest of the cruise. You can be more relaxed now that all danger is past. All the unpleasant arrangements concerning the ... er ... victims, will be taken care of as unobtrusively as possible.'

He might as well not have spoken, for the young couple could not take their eyes off one another, and Leonie's doting parents simply stared at them, smiling fondly. The captain looked at the handsome pair, whose eyes were flashing a message that required no code book to decipher. Then he added, with the smallest of smiles, knowing he was talking to himself, 'And I try to be philosophical about things, no matter how bad, believing that something good will come out of them.'

He was being heard after all, for Leonie flushed crimson.

Irish kept his face perfectly blank as he held out his free hand to Leonie, ignoring the captain's obvious remark and the Warwicks' fatuous smiles. 'Come on, Leonie,' he said, his lips twitching. 'Let's get back on deck. We have a lot to talk about.'

Photoset, printed and bound in Great Britain by
REDWOOD PRESS LIMITED, Melksham, Wiltshire